Cry of the Norwolf

To Tallulah,

Enjoy the adventure!

with best wishes

Winterscar
(The Frozen Forest)

Bear's Ridge

Signal Platform

Firehawk Nest

Giant's Cave

The Crossing

Waterfalls

River

Split Oak

The Settlement

Hunting Trails

The Winterscar Chronicles: 1

Cry
of the
Norwolf

archetype books

First published in Great Britain in 2021 by Archetype Books.

A CIP record of this book is available from the British Library.

ISBN 978-1-9997637-8-7

Printed and bound in Great Britain by Clays Ltd, Elcograf S.p.A.

Set in Adobe Garamond, 12/19pt

Follow Ian Young: winterscar.co.uk

Archetype Books
Clarendon House, 52 Cornmarket Street, Oxford, OX1 3HJ

archetypebooks.net
info@archetypebooks.net
t: @books_archetype
f: @ArchetypeBooksLtd
I: archetypebooks

FSC
www.fsc.org
MIX
Paper from
responsible sources
FSC® C018072

Archetype Books is committed to supporting local economies and businesses with genuine concern for the environment. Clays, our UK printer, is ISO14001 compliant, using 100% renewable electricity and recycling 98% of their waste.

In loving memory of Wilf 'Bagar' Mitchell

Part 1

Rescue

Arkyn tumbled to a stop about twenty paces short of the split oak. He lay on the ground staring up at the sky. The sun was shining into his eyes and all he could hear was laughing. The two girls exploded from their hiding place behind the oak tree, giggling hysterically. Arkyn peered in the direction of the laughter, brushing a long strand of straw-coloured hair from his eyes. Alys and Senni, he thought.

'Got you!' they chanted, over and over again. 'Got you!'

Arkyn rolled onto one side and got up slowly. His whole body ached. His head was spinning, but he did his best to scowl.

'That was amazing Ark!' Senni said, still laughing. 'You *flew*. You were like a giant storm eagle.'

'Yeah,' agreed Alys, with a dry smile. 'A fledgling, though. Definitely your first flight.'

Arkyn's friend, Garran, caught up and slapped him hard on his back. The boys were roughly the same height, but Garran's broad shoulders and heavy-set limbs made him seem shorter.

'Wow!' he cried. 'That was incredible! You must have flown ten paces.'

Arkyn was still dazed. He stared hard at the patch of ground where he had tripped, wondering what had happened. Then he spotted it – a thin length of cord, barely a hand's width above the ground. Hard to see from any distance, especially running as fast as he was. Only the tip of Arkyn's foot had caught the cord, but it was enough. He rubbed his sore head and smiled weakly. He had to admit it had been well hidden.

'All right,' he said to the girls. 'You got me. But what are you doing out here?'

Alys smiled. 'You first,' she said. 'Who gave *you* permission? No one is allowed out of the settlement without asking.'

Arkyn and Garran glared at her, their faces flushing.

'What do you care?' sneered Garran.

'Ha! I knew it!' said Senni with a mischievous grin. She loved winding Garran up. 'You shouldn't be out here any more than us,' she said, triumphant. 'I bet you haven't told anyone.'

Arkyn bent down to brush the dirt off his clothes. He sighed wearily. 'What do you want then?'

'We just wondered where you were going,' said Alys. 'We thought we might come too.'

'No way,' cried Garran.

'Why not?'

'It's too dangerous,' he said. 'And too far. We have to be back before sunset. And you'd slow us down.'

Senni stepped forward and jabbed Garran's chest with her finger. 'That's rubbish, and you know it is. Nobody knows these woods better than we do.'

She was right. The girls spent more time outside the settlement than any of them. Their mother was a healer. She roamed the forests collecting plants and flowers. She nearly always took the girls with her.

'All right,' agreed Arkyn, ignoring Garran's furious stare. 'You can come.' He looked back towards the settlement where thin wisps of wood smoke spiralled into the sky from

11

several roofs. He wondered whether his father, Hanserik, was awake. Unlikely, he thought. It was almost the height of the growing season, the time his mother had died. It had been several years now, but Arkyn knew that he wouldn't see much of his father during this time. Hanserik tended to sit up through the night, 'guarding the fire' he had called it. If he slept at all, it was during the day. It made no sense to Arkyn, but that was how it was.

The pit of his stomach felt hollow, but it wasn't hunger. Maybe they should have told someone where they were going after all? Hanserik wouldn't have cared, but Garran's father, Dorregan, was a different matter. Dorregan was chief of the settlement, and notorious for his hot temper. If they weren't back on time he was likely to beat them all.

Arkyn turned back to the others. 'We've got to hurry.'

'All right then,' said Alys, 'what are we waiting for?'

He shrugged and kicked off into a sprint. Fine, he thought, let's see how quickly you can run through the woods.

***

Arkyn set a fast pace, dodging trees and leaping over roots. He had only been to the hollow once before. Even then he had found it by chance. But he was confident he could get there again. The route from the split oak to the clearing was easy to follow. After that, there was the long, winding climb up the white rocks to the signal platform. From there, though, it would get harder.

The signal platform was perched on a cliff. From its front edge the rocks fell away steeply, as if they had been sliced apart by an enormous blade. Arkyn could scramble down the slope by himself, just. But he wasn't sure all four of them would manage it, there was no obvious route for them to follow. People rarely went down there.

Once upon a time, long before Arkyn was born, intrepid families had scrambled down those cliffs. They had travelled deep into the forest below in search of new land to cultivate. But the further they went into the forest, the colder it got. The land was gripped by continual winter. Those that returned spoke of never-ending snowstorms, of an endless forest scarred by ice and frost. The Frozen Forest, they called it. Where only the toughest could survive.

Arkyn and his friends were raised on tales of the Frozen Forest. There had been a settlement there once, they were told. No one really knew how many people lived there now. Arkyn had never been able to shake the feeling that, one day, he would enter the Frozen Forest.

There was no point in thinking about that now. Finding the hollow again was enough of a challenge for today.

Alys and Senni were running close behind, almost breathing down his neck. Their natural speed always took him by surprise. They seemed to move without effort, skipping over the woodland hurdles like young deer.

It had always struck him as odd that Alys and Senni were twins. Alys was only slightly older (by the time it took a pan of water to boil, so the story went) but they could hardly have been less alike. Alys had long black hair and dark, chestnut-brown eyes that seemed to study everything in great detail. She was nimble-footed and quick-witted, and Arkyn reckoned it was worth paying attention when she spoke up. Senni, on the other hand, had come into the world with a mop of curly white hair and bright blue eyes that laughed at everything they saw. To be fair, she was fast on her feet like Alys, but her tendency to blurt out the first thing that came into her head often got her into trouble.

He could hear Garran further back, heavy-footed and gasping for air, sweeping branches aside noisily. Arkyn smiled. Garran could be such an oaf.

'Ark, wait!' Garran shouted. He sounded a bit angry. But that was nothing unusual. The pair of them had been locking horns for as long as Arkyn could remember. They were more like reluctant brothers than true friends. Their fathers had grown up together, and so it seemed natural that Arkyn and Garran would do the same. They had been thrown together almost from the moment they could crawl. Now the boys had ten winters behind them and had developed a fierce rivalry.

He pushed himself harder, swinging his arms and lengthening his stride. He could feel himself breathing harder and harder, right down into his lungs. He was a galloping horse. He was an antelope in full flight. He could go on forever.

Suddenly Arkyn was alert. He felt the danger before he saw it. There were dark shapes further ahead – a flash of movement between some distant trees. They needed to hide. He slipped beneath a thick canopy of ferns and the twins followed him without a word. They had all sensed something was wrong. The twins pulled Garran in as he caught up.

'Hey,' he cried. 'What's going on?'

'Shh!' Arkyn cupped his hand over Garran's mouth and whispered. 'Someone's coming.'

***

There were six of them. Two men leading the way, four others following, walking close together, carrying two long poles on their shoulders. Strung up between the poles was a carcass. It was so big the men seemed to be struggling with the load. Arkyn couldn't get a proper look. Was it a bear maybe? No. The fur was the wrong colour. Arkyn guessed the animal might have been white once. It was hard to tell, with so much mud and blood.

He crouched as low as he could. The ferns provided a dark, shady refuge. He felt the solid, urgent thudding of his heart against his knees. The others were lined up behind him, waiting to hear what was going on.

Alys nudged his heel with her foot.

'What's happening?' she whispered.

'Yeah,' added Senni, a bit too loudly, 'I can't see a thing back here.'

'Hunters,' Arkyn whispered back. He leaned forward to

get a closer look at what they had caught. Whatever it was, it must have been heavy.

The men drew closer then suddenly stopped. Arkyn held his breath. He turned around and put a finger to his lips, his eyes locking on Garran's. Don't say anything, he implored silently. Garran stared back, frowning. He looked cross. Not now, Arkyn thought, don't start an argument now.

The men holding the poles had stopped to switch sides. The two at the back were changing places with the leaders. Arkyn finally got a clear view. He felt his heart beat even faster.

He turned back to the others. Their faces fixed on him. His mouth felt suddenly dry. His eyes were wide with shock.

'I think it's a norwolf,' he said at last.

***

Arkyn saw the colour drain from Garran's face. The twins gasped in unison and shuffled forward to try to get a better look.

'Stop it,' Arkyn whispered. 'You'll push me over.'

'How do you know it's a norwolf?' demanded Alys. 'It might just be an ordinary wolf.'

'Have a look yourself,' Arkyn said. 'It's too big for an ordinary wolf. The fur is the right colour too.'

He dropped to his knee so that Alys could sneak forward. Senni looked angry, but she let her sister take the front spot.

Alys inched forward slowly, taking care not to rustle the ferns they were hiding under. She peered through the leaves, silent for a moment.

'Wow!' she said at last. 'It's massive. And its fur is pure white.'

'Told you,' said Arkyn. 'All white, except for the face. See the black marks around the eyes and nose? Only norwolves have that.'

Alys dropped her head and crouched lower. 'Watch out,' she warned. 'They're moving again.'

The others followed her lead, staying as still as stone. Arkyn noticed the strong, male smell as the hunters walked past. It reminded him of his father.

He recognized the men's faces but couldn't name them. Then they were gone, padding quietly through the trees and down towards the settlement. Perhaps this was a blessing, thought Arkyn. There would be huge excitement when the hunters returned with their catch. A norwolf kill was a great occasion. Garran's father would surely call for a feast. All of which would mean less chance that they would be missed.

Arkyn released a long, slow breath. Then he had an awful thought. 'Does this mean there are norwolves round here?'

'Of course not,' said Senni. 'Those men will have been hunting far from here. They probably went right into the Frozen Forest.'

'Senni's right,' nodded her sister. 'You don't get norwolves down here.'

Garran didn't look so sure. 'I saw those men leave the settlement just a couple of days ago,' he said. 'It takes more than two days to get to the Frozen Forest. And it takes longer than that to track and catch a norwolf.'

Arkyn knew he was probably right. Garran's father was obsessed with hunting norwolves and he enjoyed telling his young son how it was done. The four stared at one another for a few moments, saying nothing.

'Maybe you've mixed them up with someone else,' suggested Arkyn. 'There are plenty of hunters leaving the settlement at the moment.'

Garran shook his head. 'I recognise those men. They hunt with my father. I'm sure they've only been away for two days.'

'There must be another explanation,' insisted Alys.

'She's right,' agreed Arkyn. 'Norwolves hardly ever leave the Frozen Forest. It's not cold enough for them here.'

Garran shivered and stomped his feet on the hard ground. They all knew that the first snows were due at any moment. 'Feels pretty cold to me,' he said. He picked up a small stone and flung it with all his might at a nearby tree. He missed and let out a hollow laugh.

Arkyn took a deep breath, noticing the chill air in his lungs for the first time. He had to agree that it was getting colder. Maybe even cold enough for a wandering norwolf mother, desperate to find food for her pup. Maybe it wasn't such a good idea to be out on their own. A large grey cloud passed across the sun and the wood was suddenly cast into shadow.

'My father says an adult male norwolf can grow bigger than a horse.'

'That's nonsense, Garran,' said Senni. 'Your father told you those stories to frighten you.' She was doing her best to look as if she didn't believe him, but her eyes were like full moons. Arkyn, too, was troubled by visions of norwolves killing the settlement workhorses with a single blow of their massive paws.

'Think it's rubbish?' Garran challenged. 'He's got a scar across his back that's as long as my arm.'

'And I suppose you're going tell us he killed it with his bare hands,' Alys said with a mocking laugh.

'Of course he didn't,' said Garran. 'Everyone knows it takes at least four true arrows to stop an adult norwolf.'

Arkyn jumped up. 'Come on,' he said. 'We're wasting time. Even if they *did* kill a norwolf near here it's dead now. So there's nothing to worry about. If we're going to get back to the settlement while it's still light we need to get a move on.'

The twins stood up straight away. 'We're ready.'

Alys said, 'You still haven't told us where we're going.'

'You'll like it,' said Arkyn, grinning. 'It's great for back-flips.'

The three of them looked down at Garran, who hadn't moved.

'You coming?' said Arkyn. More a challenge than a question. Garran got up slowly wearing a deep, thoughtful frown.

'Yeah,' he said slowly, 'I'm coming.'

***

The sun was at its highest when they reached the signal platform. They had all been there before, several times, but it always took their breath away. They were at the very top of the forest.

'We've made good time,' Arkyn said as they climbed the final few paces.

He stood on the platform's sturdy wooden stage, surveying the small two-man shelter and central firepit and wondering why nobody stayed up here anymore. The platform was as old as the settlement itself and, in the early days, people would take turns to live here. Their job was to watch for gathering rain or snow storms, or even for signs of fire when the forest was dry and the weather very warm. Then they would light a beacon to warn the settlement down in the valley. But that custom had stopped long before Arkyn was born.

They sat down to rest. Senni dipped into her small canvas shoulder bag and pulled out a handful of food. Nuts and berries, mostly, and a few strips of dried meat. She shared it out with Alys and Garran while Arkyn walked over to the edge of the platform and looked over.

The slope was littered with scree and broken roots, leading down to the tree canopy. The descent was steeper than he remembered. There was no usable route down, not even a hint of one. He felt a pang of anxiety. Perhaps this wasn't such a good idea after all, but if he pulled out now Garran would never let him forget it.

The others wandered across to join him, their fingertips and lips black with berry juice.

'It's that way,' he announced, trying to sound relaxed as he pointed down the slope and into the forest.

Senni peered over the edge. 'Are you sure?' she said. 'I don't see a way down.'

'That's mad,' declared Alys. She leaned forward, steadying herself against Senni. 'We'd just slide down the cliff.'

'I promise you it's worth it,' said Arkyn.

'What can be worth going down there for? We'll kill ourselves.'

'Yeah, Ark,' said Garran. 'What's the big deal?'

Arkyn was silent for a moment. He could see he was going to have to tell them. 'I found a hollow down there,' he said at last. 'It's huge. And it's full of leaves and moss. Soft as a bed. You can climb the trees around it and jump straight in. It's fantastic.'

He could tell from their faces that they were interested. But there was still the problem of the slope.

'It sounds fun,' agreed Senni. 'But there's no way down.'

'I've done it before.' He decided not to tell them how hard it was, or how scared he had been.

'Really?' said Garran. Arkyn could tell he was doubtful. 'Where did you start from?'

He pointed to a root that was poking out of the slope. 'There. You climb down the root and slide a bit. There's another one further down. There are places where you can stop yourself falling.' He paused as he tried to remember where those places were. 'They're just not very clear from here,' he said at last.

Garran whistled under his breath. 'Well,' he said, 'perhaps you can show us the way.'

Arkyn paused again. He looked at Garran and smiled.

'Happy to,' he said at last. He walked across to a spot just above the root and sat down, hanging his legs over the edge. Then he lowered himself onto the root, using first his legs and then his arms to drop further down the slope. The others watched with interest.

'So,' said Senni, 'now that you're hanging from a root, what do you do next?'

Arkyn looked up at them. He was grinning, sort of. 'Er… I think I'll swing across to that one over there.' The tiny stub was barely bigger than a hand.

'You can't get a hold on that,' said Alys. 'It's too small.'

'It'll be fine,' he said. 'I'm sure it held me before.'

Arkyn reached out with his feet, swinging back slightly, and then forward. Each time, his legs swung closer to the tiny root. On the third attempt he got a foot on it. He grabbed another branch to steady himself, but it came out of the earth like a young weed.

Arkyn fell so quickly he didn't have time to shout out. He dropped like a stone, kicking up clouds of dust as he slid down the slope. He heard the screams of the others. As he fell, he tried to grab at other roots, but missed them all. The forest was rising up to meet him.

***

Incredibly, it was a soft landing. In fact, everything about the fall was soft. The rocks had smooth edges. There were no painful thorns on the bushes. Even the ground was layered with a thick bed of mulch. He found himself cradled in a nest of grass and leaves. He had been lucky.

He lay still for a few seconds, taking deep breaths, staring up at the leafy canopy he had just fallen through. He could hardly believe it. Had he really fallen that far? And he was fine, wasn't he? He wriggled his fingers slowly. They were all there. He tried raising his arms slightly. A bit stiff, but basically fine. He turned his feet from side to side. He tried raising each leg, one at a time. Amazing, he thought. There was no pain.

He pushed himself up onto his elbows, and that was when he realized there was something wrong. Not with his body, but with the space around him. It wasn't something he saw or heard. It wasn't even a smell. It was instinct. A warning bell in his head telling him that he wasn't alone.

An animal lay half-buried in the leaves. Its head and body were hidden, but two dark eyes were looking at him. Arkyn stayed completely still, holding his breath. There was a slight rustling as leaves dropped from the creature's head. For the second time that day, Arkyn's mouth turned dry.

It was a norwolf.

It stared at him.

Arkyn stared back. He couldn't move a muscle. It was as if someone had flicked a switch and turned him off. His thoughts were whirling out of control. I'm done for. It will tear me to pieces.

Somewhere in the distance he could hear voices calling his name.

Slowly, very slowly, Arkyn began to breathe again. His mouth slightly open. He allowed the air to escape, softly and quietly. He didn't want to make any sudden noises. He breathed in. The air moved through his body, giving him life. He started to feel calmer. If this was a norwolf why hadn't it moved? Why hadn't it attacked him straight away?

He slowly looked around. They were in some kind of pit. It was deep, but quite narrow. If this was a small space, he reasoned, then this must be a small norwolf. That made sense didn't it? He closed his mouth and breathed through his nose. Bigger breaths. Deeper.

He let his eyes move along the body of the animal from head to tail. It was a bit like stroking it, only he was using his eyes. He wondered what he would do if the beast suddenly jumped at him.

The closer he looked, the more he realised that it was no bigger than a fox cub. But it was clearly a norwolf. He could tell from the black marks on its face and the large, broad ears. Its fur was more grey than white, though. Must be a baby, he thought. A young norwolf pup. No more than a few weeks old.

Still it didn't move. Maybe it was as scared as he was. Those large, black eyes stared back at him, hardly blinking.

'Hey,' said Arkyn in a soft voice. 'Are you all right?'

Then the sounds started. They were soft at first, but quickly grew louder. Arkyn had heard music before, many times. People on the settlement made music. They strummed and plucked strings; they beat drums and blew into long, beautifully carved flutes. And they sang of course. But they never made sounds like this.

It was like an army invading his ears. Scratching and scraping, banging and thumping, hooting and whistling. It rose and fell in pitch and volume, first a whisper and then a scream. His head was filled with it. He covered his ears with the palms of his hands, but that just made the noise worse. It bellowed at him and fought him off like an angry child.

'Stop it!' Arkyn gasped. He didn't know who he was talking to, but he had to do something. He looked at the norwolf pup. Those eyes were still staring at him. The awful clamour in his ears faded, like a wave dropping back from the shore. There was a moment of silence. Then a single, quiet voice in his head.

Help, it said.

***

'Who's there?' Arkyn looked around to see where the voice had come from.

Sore, it said.

Arkyn kept searching for the person who had spoken. 'What do you mean "saw"?' he said. Then the sound returned. It built in his head like a distant storm. 'No, no,' he cried. 'Go away…'

Strangely, the sound seemed to obey. But the voice returned in its place.

Help, it said again. It was a young voice, and it sounded scared.

'How can I help you?' Arkyn replied, looking all around. 'I can't see you.'

Here, it said. *In front of you.*

Arkyn turned to the pup.

Sore, the voice repeated. Arkyn found himself looking at the norwolf's mouth, to see whether it had moved. I'm going mad, he thought. *Of course it's not the pup. I must have knocked my head when I fell.*

The norwolf's mouth was slightly open. It was gently panting. *Sore*, the voice in his head insisted. *Need help.*

Arkyn raised himself so that he was sitting. He noticed a few cuts on his elbows and knees.

The sound in his head rumbled on quietly in the background. He stared at the norwolf, feeling quite calm now. Curious, even. He found himself staring deep into the animal's eyes. Then, for no particular reason, he tried saying *Need help?* but without speaking the words. He simply thought the words in his head, while watching the animal closely. For a few moments he heard nothing, just gentle rumbling. Then he heard the young voice again.

Hurts, it said.

It was so obvious, and so surprising, that he almost laughed out loud. *Of course it's not speaking. It's an animal. It's thinking. Don't speak to it. Think to it.*

He was surprised how easily this came to him. It felt much the same as normal thinking. The main difference was that he tried not to have lots of other thoughts at once. Instead, he focused on a single message. That part was hard because other thoughts kept popping into his head, like whether or not the norwolf was going to turn on him.

What do you need? he thought.

Cannot move, the voice said.

Arkyn looked at the norwolf again, his eyes wide. He was scarcely able to believe what was happening. He glanced at the animal's legs. Its front legs looked fine as far as he could see. The back ones were hidden under leaves. He focused his thoughts again. This time he held the norwolf's gaze.

Where is the pain? he asked.

Under the leaves.

Arkyn moved slowly. He stretched his arm out until he could reach the leaves that had fallen across the pup's back. He could hardly believe that he was getting so close. The pup's eyes followed him closely, but it still didn't move.

Arkyn gently brushed the leaves away, trying hard not to touch the animal itself. He didn't want to cause more pain. The leaves were wet and sticky, as if it had been raining. Then Arkyn realised it wasn't water. It was blood.

The wound was long but not deep – a hunting knife was the most likely cause. Arkyn sat back and took a deep breath. He didn't know what to do. The pup was watching him closely.

Help, came the voice again.

I don't know how to help you. I'm stuck here too.

Help.

Just wait. I need to time to think. He paused for a moment, before adding. *Are you really talking to me?*

Help.

Arkyn sighed deeply. It was bad enough to have fallen so far and to end up in some kind of hole with a norwolf. But what was going on in his head? Were they really talking to each other?

He looked again at the animal's wound. It wasn't bleeding now. Maybe it just needed a bandage of some kind. The twins would know what to do. The twins. And Garran. It was the first time that he had thought about them.

***

'Arkyn!'

Alys sounded close. Arkyn looked up. Leaves and branches blocked his view of the sky. He got up onto his knees, moving slowly so as not to alarm the norwolf. Then he tried standing up. He felt wobbly on his feet. He tried to reach up but the branches were too far away.

'Down here!' he shouted back.

'OK,' cried Alys, 'I'm coming. Garran, drop me a bit more.'

There was a rustling sound above him. A pair of feet pushed their way through the greenery. Then a pair of legs appeared above him, hanging in the air.

'You all right?' she called down. There was a thick rope coiled around her waist. Arkyn guessed that Garran and Senni must be at the other end.

'Yeah, think so.'

'That was some fall.'

'Yeah.' He looked at the rope. 'I could have done with that earlier.'

'Can you believe it? It was hidden under the platform.'

She dropped down onto the ground next to Arkyn, then looked up and shouted: 'That's far enough. I'm with him.'

'Is he OK?' shouted Garran.

'I'm fine,' Arkyn called back.

'You're not fine,' Garran replied with a laugh. 'You're crazy.'

Arkyn smiled. Not crazy, he thought. Just a bit too curious maybe. He turned to Alys. She hadn't noticed the pup yet. 'Look,' he said, pointing to the animal curled up in the corner.

Alys took in a sharp breath and jumped up into a crouch, ready to defend herself.

'Is that a norwolf?'

'Yeah, it's a pup. But it can't move. It's hurt... look at the leg.'

She relaxed and leaned forward to get a closer look.

'Oh, I see now.' She studied the bloody wound with grim interest.

'What do you think we should do?' he asked.

'Do?' She sounded surprised. 'Leave it of course. Those hunters we saw must have caught its mother.'

'But it will starve to death. Unless something else kills it first.'

'So?' She gave him a baffled look. 'It's a norwolf, Arkyn,' she said simply. 'We mustn't help it.'

'But it's just a pup.'

'Yeah… and a pup will grow into an adult. You saw the size of the mother.' She looked across at the animal lying in the leaves. It had tried to move when she first appeared, but it didn't have enough strength. 'Maybe we should just finish it off ourselves,' she said.

Arkyn was surprised. She and Senni were always rescuing injured creatures. It seemed odd that she would suggest killing this one. But norwolves had a strange effect on people. Many said they were cursed. How did the saying go? 'Norwolves move in darkness, and darkness follows them wherever they go.' He looked back at the wounded creature lying on its bloody bed of leaves. Its eyes watched him silently. No sign of darkness there.

Something grew within him. It was a strange feeling. Exciting but also daunting. He knew what he was going to do.

'No,' he said finally. 'We're going to help it.' He watched as Alys started to unwind the rope from her waist. She didn't think he was being serious.

'Come on,' she said. 'The fall's made you a bit crazy, that's all. We can't do anything for it, even if we wanted to.' She handed him the rope. 'If we went anywhere near the settlement with it, people would kill it on the spot. And Garran's dad would skin us alive too,' she added.

But Arkyn was insistent. 'We can hide it and take care of it,' he said, his voice firm. 'Your mother will have something for the wound.'

Alys put the rope down and looked at him. Her face was caked in dirt and dust but he could see the shock in her eyes.

'You're really serious?'

'Absolutely.'

'And what do we do when it's well enough to move? Norwolf pups kill children too, you know.'

'Not this one.'

'How do you know?'

'I just know… It won't hurt us.'

Alys forced a laugh. 'You got some special magic then?'

She was poking fun at him and he had to be careful what he said. He didn't want her to know about the voices. Not yet anyway. 'I just know it'll be all right.' He leaned across to the pup.

Alys gasped. 'Wait, Arkyn.' He could hear the worry in her voice, but he ignored it. Instead, he directed all his energy into a single message for the norwolf.

I'm going to pick you up, he thought. *I'm going to help you.*

Help, came the familiar reply.

***

The cry of the norwolf, frightened and alone, had changed Arkyn's world. *He* had changed. He could feel it in his heart.

Back on the signal platform, Garran was just the same. Arkyn knew that he wouldn't agree to help rescue the norwolf. But he hadn't expected him to pull out his knife the moment he saw it.

'We're going to kill it, right?' he said. He held the knife as if ready to strike. His eyes were fierce and determined. Arkyn pushed him away, holding the animal awkwardly in the crook of his arm.

'Don't you dare,' he shouted.

Garran stumbled back, surprised. His cheeks flooded red with anger. 'Are you mad? It would kill us without a thought.'

'Just leave it alone.' Arkyn turned away from Garran, shielding the animal in his arms. 'It's only a pup. It won't hurt us.'

'Maybe not now, but one day…'

'You lay one finger on it and I'll…' He didn't finish the sentence. He didn't really know what he would do. But he knew the strength of this feeling was real. He would do whatever it took to protect the norwolf. He turned and walked across the signal platform to the path that led back down to the settlement.

Arkyn climbed down from the platform with the injured animal in Senni's pack, slung across his back.

Senni, meanwhile, stuck to his heels like a puppy. She fussed around the half-open bag, trying to catch glimpses of the norwolf's smooth, pale grey fur and pointed ears. Arkyn had forgotten about her weakness for vulnerable creatures. Even a norwolf didn't worry her.

'Just leave it alone,' said Alys. 'It's not going to get any better if you keep poking your nose in there. You're just making it stressed.'

Arkyn could tell she wasn't happy about any of this. And she had a point. After all, why save a norwolf? They were known killers, feared by humans across the land. They were major trophies for hunters. But this one was different. Arkyn knew he couldn't tell any of them what had happened in the pit. All he knew was that he had to save it. From time to time he glanced back at Garran trudging along behind them in silence, his head down.

'I can't believe that this sweet little thing is going to grow into a full-size norwolf,' said Senni, still peering into the sack on Arkyn's back and making clucking noises to try and keep it calm. 'It's impossible to imagine, isn't it?'

'You can ask my father about that,' said Garran suddenly. 'I reckon he can imagine it pretty well.'

In all the excitement, Arkyn hadn't really thought about Dorregan. Would Garran tell his father about the norwolf? He felt a sickly, nervous sensation in his stomach. For the first time in his life he wondered whether he would be able to trust Garran to keep a secret.

'Where are we going to take it then?' said Alys at last, looking at Arkyn. 'What's your plan?'

'There's a cave near here,' he replied. 'Garran and I used to play there when we were younger.'

'Are you talking about Giant's Cave?' Garran said. 'That's no good now. It collapsed last winter. There's nothing there but crumbled rock.'

Arkyn looked at Garran. They shared many memories of Giant's Cave – of secret meetings and mock battles. He knew as well as Garran that the cave had collapsed. They had both felt sorrow at the loss of their special place.

'Which is why it's perfect,' Arkyn replied. 'No one goes there any more. It's an ideal place to hide the pup.'

'It's quite close to the settlement,' said Garran. 'You not think about that?'

'Of course I did. It'll make it easier to take food and stuff.'

'And easier for someone else to find it.'

'Only if one of us tells.'

They walked on in silence, each lost in their own thoughts.

'I won't tell anyone,' said Senni suddenly. 'I promise.'

'Nor will I,' said Alys.

The three of them turned to Garran. He had picked up a long, whip-like stick and was beating the side of trees as they walked.

'Yeah all right,' he said, his eyes distant. 'I'll keep it to myself.'

Arkyn nodded his thanks.

'I'm not looking after it though,' Garran went on. 'I want nothing to do with it.'

'That's fine,' said Senni brightly. 'We know what it needs anyway, don't we Alys?'

'Honey to treat the wound,' said Alys, 'and a bandage with marigold leaves. That's what I'd do anyway.'

'And we can feed it dried meat from the kennel stores,' said Senni. 'No one will miss a few strips.'

'Can you get all that without your mother finding out?'

'Oh yes,' said Alys quickly. 'She goes into the woods most mornings, or she's out visiting sick people. We can get things then.'

'What about when the wound is better?' said Senni. 'The pup will want to move around won't it? It might try to get away.' She peered into the bag once more. The norwolf's eyes were closed. 'What are we going to do then?'

'Exactly,' said Garran in a grim voice. 'It won't last a

morning if anyone finds it near the settlement. And it has no mother to protect it.' Arkyn wished Garran would shut up, especially if he wasn't going to help. He didn't say anything though because he knew Garran was right. He was carrying a norwolf on his back, after all. A fierce and deadly creature that would grow into a killer. Yet he didn't care. It was almost as if he didn't think of it as a norwolf anymore. How could that be? He had heard its voice, hadn't he? Or had it all been his imagination? He had certainly heard *something*. Whatever it was, he knew he couldn't ignore the cry for help.

And then there were the strange sounds in his head. They were still there, still playing quietly in the background. Would they simply fade away, he wondered, or was he stuck with them?

✳✳✳

Arkyn felt his anxiety grow as they walked through the woods. The straps of the pack dug painfully into his shoulders. The warmth of the animal's body against his back made him sweat and itch. Worst of all was the smell of wounded flesh and bloody fur. He moved slowly between the trees, fearing every noisy footfall. If they met any hunters then it would all be over. The norwolf would be killed. He stopped and looked at the others. He lowered his voice almost to a whisper.

'I think we should split up.'

'Fine by me,' replied Garran. Arkyn wasn't surprised that Garran agreed so quickly, but he felt sad. He had hoped he might offer to stay. But Garran hadn't even bothered to lower his voice. Arkyn could see he was fed up and wanted to get back to the settlement as quickly as possible.

Alys and Senni looked more worried.

'Are you sure that's a good idea?' whispered Senni. 'What if you run into someone?'

'It's better if I'm alone. I'll make less noise, and it's easier to hide if I need to.'

'He's right,' agreed Alys. 'If three of us head back to the settlement now then we're less likely to be missed by anyone. And we can meet you at Giant's Cave later.'

'Not me,' said Garran.

Senni gave Garran a dark look. 'Well yeah, obviously not you,' she snapped. Arkyn couldn't resist a small smile. Senni was never one to hide her feelings. She obviously thought Garran was a traitor. Garran's face flushed slightly but he made no comment. Instead he turned and stalked off through the woods, heading for the settlement.

'See you later,' called Arkyn. Garran didn't turn around. He just waved a hand and kept walking. He and Garran often fought about things but their arguments never lasted long. This felt different. Arkyn *knew* he was doing the right thing. He could feel it. Trouble was, he was sure Garran felt just as strongly as he did.

'Better off without him I reckon,' remarked Senni.

Alys nodded. 'Yeah. I just hope he doesn't go running to his father.'

'He wouldn't do that,' Arkyn said quietly. He realised as he spoke the words that he wasn't sure he believed them. He looked up through the trees and shivered. A grey blanket of cloud was forming above them, and a chill breeze was building. He felt a sudden sense of urgency.

'I'm going straight down from here,' he said, pointing to an unlikely looking route through the trees. Somewhere down below he could hear the thrumming beat of the river.

He turned to Alys. 'Are you sure you can get the supplies and get back to the cave in good time? We need to be back home before it gets dark.'

Senni sniggered. 'You all right Arkyn? Not feeling a bit

nervous by any chance?' Arkyn noted the look of challenge in her eyes.

'Course not,' he protested. He could feel his cheeks blushing. 'It's just…' He struggled to find the words. If he was feeling scared he definitely wasn't going to admit it. 'It's just if we're late back then it'll be noticed.'

Alys patted him on the shoulder then she and Senni set off down the path. 'Don't worry,' she said. 'We'll find you in plenty of time.'

Arkyn watched as they disappeared between the trees, following the route Garran had taken. A few moments later he heard a scream: 'Tiri-meee!' It was the hunters' cry. He froze on the spot. He didn't dare to breathe. Then he heard Senni laughing. Slowly, he relaxed again. Smiled. Senni could be a bit annoying, but he had to admit she had a good hunting call.

✳✳✳

Arkyn traced the edge of the wood as far as the river. Then he walked up towards the first waterfall. It was a simple climb from there to the place they knew as Giant's Cave. It was an old name. There was no giant of course, but everyone knew it as that and the name had never died out.

A fallen tree had caused most of the damage to the cave. Roots that had gripped the slope above had finally run out of earth to cling to. The trunk and all its branches had come crashing down across the entrance. Much of the rocky mouth had also crumbled. It was as if the giant had been gagged. But there was still a way in. You just needed to look carefully.

Arkyn picked up a large lump of rock and tossed it to one side. Then another and another. He worked quickly, without stopping. He felt the weight of the norwolf against his back. The heat of its body was like an oven against his skin. He was soon dripping with sweat. He didn't stop shifting stones until he had made a hole large enough to step through.

It was a relief to clamber into the cave. The air was cool and dry. Arkyn chose a rock and sat down facing out towards

45

the sun. He noted its position in the sky. Would there be enough time for the twins to get here before night came? There was no point in worrying about that. He had more important things to do now. He turned back to the cave, searching for a spot where he could settle the norwolf.

He found the perfect place, a small ledge in the wall of the cave, about the height of his shoulder. It was like a nest in the rocks, big enough to hold a small animal and high enough to avoid most dangers.

Arkyn was still a little afraid of touching the norwolf. He and Garran had been trapping small animals for as long as he could remember. But never anything bigger than a squirrel or a rabbit. A norwolf was very different, even one as small as this. And he hadn't touched it since carefully lowering it into Senni's bag.

He slipped the bag off his back, moving very slowly, and gently laid it on the ledge. Then he lifted the flap of the bag and peered in. There was the strong smell of animal, of dried blood and dirt. The norwolf's eyes stared back at him, unblinking. Arkyn noted that there was no fear in those eyes, no fear at all.

***

'Ark? You in there?'

'Yeah, over here.'

'Where?'

'Here…'

It took a few moments for the twins to pick him out. That was a good sign. He and the norwolf were well hidden.

Alys carried a leather bag over her shoulder. It smelled of dried meat.

'There were two births last night,' said Alys. 'Mother's been sleeping all afternoon. I've got honey, and some marigold paste for the cut.' She looked up to the ledge where Arkyn had settled the norwolf. 'How's he doing?'

'OK I think. He paused for a moment. You reckon it's a boy, then?'

'No idea.'

'Have you not worked that out yet?'

'Course not.'

'Shall we find out?'

'I don't know. Does it really matter?'

'Well… Either way, it's going to grow stronger than any of us. I suppose a girl might be a bit easier to handle.'

The three of them stared at the little pile of fur lying on the ledge. Its breath was steady and calm. Its eyes alert and curious. Senni suddenly stepped forward between them and reached up to the ledge. She lifted the norwolf's back leg into the air.

The startled creature's tiny head darted towards Senni's hand, quick as a snake, and growled. A proper growl, too. It didn't seem possible that such a small thing could make a noise like that. They all stepped back in alarm.

'Woah!' cried Senni. Her face flushed. 'Sorry. I didn't mean to…'

'That was pretty stupid,' said Arkyn. 'Moving the wounded leg like that.'

The norwolf started licking the deep red stripe as if trying to clean the soreness away.

'Well,' said Alys. 'At least we know what we're dealing with now.'

'Yeah,' said Arkyn. He wasn't surprised. Somehow, he had known all along that it was a male. 'Right,' he said, looking at the bag Alys had brought with her. 'Shall we try and put something on the cut?'

'Sure,' she said. She pulled a tiny jar of honey out of the bag. 'You want to have a go?'

Arkyn shrugged and smiled weakly. He took the jar and held it up in the air. Then he turned it on its side to test how quickly the honey came out.

The norwolf had stopped licking the wound and was watching him very carefully. Arkyn turned to face the animal. He wanted to say something to it to calm him down. But he was also aware of Alys and Senni. There was no way he could try talking to him while they were here. What if something went wrong? They would think he was mad. But he didn't need to worry. The norwolf spoke first.

What are you going to do?

Arkyn wanted to laugh out loud when he heard the voice in his head again. It gave him such sudden joy. It was both a new and an old feeling, a bit like finding a new hiding place, then remembering you had known it all along but had forgotten it. He relaxed. He knew he was safe. He focused his thoughts, ignoring the girls standing behind him.

I'm going to put some medicine on your leg, he thought. *It will help it heal.*

He drizzled the honey slowly, letting it fall in a thin trickle along the length of the open wound. The norwolf didn't flinch. He watched the liquid fall, then licked the smooth rock where it had spilled.

Senni gave a little laugh of delight. 'He likes it,' she said.

The marigold paste went on after that. Arkyn smeared it on in thick stripes with his fingers. The smell was strong and the sticky balm seemed to get everywhere, but still the norwolf didn't object.

Sore, came the voice.

I know, thought Arkyn. *But this will help. Trust me.*

A human did it.

Arkyn stopped for a moment. He wasn't sure what to say. *I'm sorry*, he thought. *Not all humans would do this.*

You wouldn't?

No… never, thought Arkyn.

What about the ones with you?

Arkyn thought of Garran drawing his knife. *No, not them either.*

He had almost finished. He didn't really know if the lotion would work, but at least the wound was protected now. Then the norwolf sent another thought.

Where is my mother?

Arkyn stopped what he was doing. He had no idea what to say. In his head, he had a very clear picture of the adult norwolf they had seen earlier. He saw its giant muzzle lolling back as it swung from the poles. He saw a long tongue flopping out of its mouth. The thought of it made him feel ashamed and disgusted. He also felt angry. The norwolf addressed him again.

You saw her.

Arkyn looked up in surprise. How did he know? Could the norwolf see what he was thinking? He hesitated for a moment.

Yes. I saw her.

The humans killed her.

Yes.

Why?

Arkyn stared at the norwolf. He felt helpless. What was there to say, apart from the truth? *Hunters killed her because they are afraid of her.* He paused for a moment. Then, he added: *And they will try to kill you too.*

✳✳✳

The norwolf's wound healed quickly. Arkyn visited the cave each morning and evening. He brought dried meat from the kennels and honey from the twins. He also brought water from the river, which he poured into a hollow on the rock ledge.

There was a change on the evening of the third day. The norwolf stood on all four legs for the first time. Arkyn was surprised how big he was. He watched as the young animal raised his head and sniffed the air. He looked towards the mouth of the cave. Outside, the light was fading. Night was coming. Arkyn knew that the norwolf wanted to leave.

The pup looked at him. The exchanges between them came easily now. The sounds in his head were still there but they were softer. He had grown weary of them. It was like a door had been opened in his mind revealing a world he didn't understand. Arkyn wasn't even sure it was a world he wanted to visit. But he was starting to think that he might have no choice. This world was coming towards him whether he liked it or not.

Want to run, thought the norwolf.

Yes, thought Arkyn. *Soon you will. Not yet.* For a brief moment he pictured them running together. What a thrill that would be! Side by side through woodland or across an open plain. They would run all day.

Ready now, replied the norwolf. Arkyn smiled. Did they share dreams as well as thoughts?

You're only just standing again.

Feel strong.

52

At least wait until it gets dark. It will be safer for you then.

Arkyn bent down to his bag for a piece of meat.

The norwolf trotted across the cave and stood at the entrance. Arkyn only turned his back for a moment. But it was long enough.

A figure jumped out of the shadows.

It rose up in front of the norwolf, an arm raised. Arkyn saw a flash of silver in the pale light. It was a blade, and he knew whose it was.

'Garran!' he shouted. 'Don't!'

Garran seemed ready to throw himself at the animal. He had painted red stripes across his cheeks and forehead, like the hunters do. He was screaming the call. Tiri-meeee… Tri-ah, tri-ah… Tiri-meee…!

Arkyn watched in horror as Garran prepared for a fight he could never hope to win.

The norwolf moved fast. He dropped down low as Garran drew near. His eyes blazed with fury. There was a rumbling growl, low and long. His fur rippled as the muscles tightened. There was no hint of fear or surprise in the beast.

Garran hesitated. His knife blade seemed to wobble in the half-darkness. Arkyn watched as Garran's eyes blinked several times. It was as if he had just woken up. Then he let his arm fall to his side and his face turned pale as milk.

'Stay where you are,' said Arkyn quickly. 'Whatever you do, don't move.' Embers of anger stirred within him. He stared at Garran. He was struggling to understand what had just happened. He knew Garran was against saving the norwolf but he never thought he would go this far. He never thought Garran would try and kill him.

Garran was breathing hard. His hand squeezed the knife until his knuckles turned white. He looked scared.

'But it's a norwolf!' he said, as if that explained everything. 'We can't let it live.'

'What's he ever done to you?' shouted Arkyn. 'Hunters killed his mother. Now he's all alone.' His strength of feeling surprised him. He wondered what would happen if he turned away, if he left Garran to defend himself. No matter how angry he was, he knew he had to help him.

The norwolf continued to stare at Garran, growling softly.

'It's too late now isn't it?' Garran sounded desperate. 'Look how angry it is. It's going to kill us both.'

'Just stay where you are. Don't do anything.'

***

Arkyn concentrated all his thoughts on the norwolf. He went looking for the sounds in his head. He didn't know what they meant, but he felt he needed to focus on them now. He needed the norwolf to listen to him. If he couldn't get through, then surely Garran was doomed.

Stop! Please stop!

To his surprise, the norwolf responded straight away.

Away! Away! came the cry. The voice was scared. It was hard to believe that it belonged to the same fierce animal that was snarling at Garran.

Yes. He is going away, thought Arkyn. *He knows he was wrong. He is my friend. He will not hurt you. He is afraid.*

Away! repeated the norwolf.

Garran hadn't moved. His arms hung limply by his side. He still had the knife, but his fingers could barely hold it. His whole body seemed in the grip of fear, as if he was held under a spell. 'Garran,' said Arkyn. 'Take a step towards me, but don't do anything sudden.'

Garran didn't budge. His eyes were fixed on the growling muzzle of the norwolf. 'Are you mad? If I move a muscle it'll pounce.'

'Trust me. You'll be all right. Come over here.'

For a few moments Garran still didn't move. Then, inch by inch, he shuffled slowly towards Arkyn.

When he reached him he dropped slowly to the ground and sat still as stone.

Arkyn sent a thought to the norwolf. *Safe now.*

The norwolf had watched Garran move across the cave. His eyes still blazed with fury and alarm. He only started to relax when the young hunter was on the floor.

For Garran, the silence was almost worse than the growling. 'What's he doing now?' he asked. 'Why is he just watching us?'

'Just shut up and wait,' snapped Arkyn. Now that Garran was safe, he was finding it difficult to hide his true feelings. The norwolf's eyes settled on Arkyn. *Need to run.*

Yes, Arkyn replied. *You need to run.*

There was no choice now. Garran was just the start, there would be others. People would come looking. He would never be safe.

The norwolf turned towards the mouth of the cave. It was not quite dark. He lifted his nose again, as if testing the air. Then he turned back to Arkyn.

The boy and the norwolf stared at each other in silence.

Then, to his surprise, the sounds returned. This time, though, it was not painful to hear. It was beautiful. It reminded him of a soft breeze whispering through the forest, where the tallest trees creak and sigh as the air presses against them. And somewhere, in the distance, the bell-like refrain of a woodland stream. It was enchanting.

For a brief moment, Arkyn wondered whether the norwolf wanted to say something. It struck him as strange, to think of an animal lost for words. Then, just as suddenly, the sounds faded and the voice came once more.

Didn't know this could happen, it said.

Arkyn smiled. *Neither did I.*

Will not forget.

No, will not forget.

The norwolf stepped easily over a branch lying across the mouth of the cave. Then he was gone.

Part 2

Firehawk

The storyteller lifted his arms towards the night sky. Then, slowly, he moved them down and back up again. Flames from the pit seemed to rise and fall in time with the slow, steady flap of his arms. Arkyn smiled to himself. He had seen this many times before, but the effect was always impressive. The storyteller was pretending that his arms were massive wings. He was the giant bird of his story. He was the firehawk.

The storyteller stood on the speaker's stone, next to the firepit. A group of young children sat in front of him. They were as still as statues. Their eyes, and a few mouths, were wide open. The broad sleeves of the storyteller's tunic threw shadows on them. They were drowning in waves of darkness and light.

In one hand the storyteller held a long wooden pole. This was the storypole. It was just as Arkyn remembered. Capped at each end with polished sleeves of bronze. A long purple scarf tied at the top. From time to time the storyteller would pound the base of the pole against the speaker's stone. The noise still made Arkyn jump.

He sat at the edge of the group with the older children, and leaned back on his elbows. He closed his eyes. How many times had he heard this story? Five? Ten? Everyone knew the tales of Raven and the firehawk. They were told in different ways but the ending was always the same. Raven was about the same age as Arkyn. She lived on a settlement in the Frozen Forest. At the start of the story, the settlement is attacked by thieves. She runs away. Then she gets lost in the forest and wanders for several days, alone and hungry.

In some versions, Raven stumbles upon a firehawk's nest. The firehawk is like a giant eagle, and it breathes fire like a dragon. In other versions of the story, the firehawk drops out of the sky and attacks her. After a while, Raven tames the firehawk and persuades it to help her.

Raven and the firehawk become friends. She chooses to

stay in the Frozen Forest. She even sleeps in the firehawk's nest. At one point (this was Arkyn's favourite part), she learns to ride on the beast's back. Then they roam the mountains and valleys, sharing many adventures.

Arkyn yawned silently. He looked across at Garran and rolled his eyes. He wanted him to think that he was bored. Garran smiled, and turned back to the storyteller. Garran loved the stories as much as he did.

The storyteller had been on the settlement for five nights. Each night during his stay he told the next part of the story. This evening the moon was full, which meant he would be leaving in the morning. The last bit of the story would be told tonight, which was why so many people had come to listen.

In the final part, Raven is running from a norwolf. The firehawk tries to save her and the norwolf turns on the bird. There is a terrible fight. As the storyteller described the battle between the two beasts, his words seemed to follow the pace of the fight. Faster and faster he spoke. His voice rose and fell as he stared into the firepit. It was as if he could see the story taking place in the flames.

Arkyn watched the faces of the people around him. Their eyes were transfixed on the storyteller. It was like they were under a spell. The fight between the norwolf and the firehawk doesn't last long. The norwolf leaps onto the firehawk's back, biting deeply into the bird's neck. Raven is helpless to prevent the death of her dear friend.

Arkyn looked around, wondering who would be the first to weep. He glanced across to Garran. His eyes were shining.

'Are you crying?' he whispered.

'Of course not,' said Garran. He blinked hard and turned his head away.

'You are!'

'I'm not. It's just a bit of smoke.'

Arkyn leaned across and gave him a playful nudge in the ribs. 'You're sad because the firehawk gets killed.'

'Of course I'm not. I told you, I got smoke in my eyes. Why would I care about a firehawk?'

'Ah, don't worry Garran. It's only a story.'

'Shut up.'

It's a stupid story anyway, thought Arkyn. A stupid, unfair story. He lay flat on his back and stared up into the night sky. He didn't want to listen anymore. He knew the rest.

Raven is so upset that she vows to hunt down and kill the norwolf herself. There is a long and exhausting hunt. She tracks the norwolf to a cave in the Frozen Forest. She sits outside the cave all night, waiting for her moment to strike. In the end, the norwolf emerges and Raven's arrow finds its mark. There are cheers and claps all round. The children scream with delight.

Everyone hates norwolves, he thought sadly. They have no idea.

***

'I think,' declared Senni, 'that of all the stories of the Frozen Forest, Raven and the firehawk is my favourite.' She paused for a moment and looked up at her sister, her eyes suddenly bright. 'Do you remember, Alys, when mother showed us how to make tiny firehawks out of bits of straw? We used to make them while she told us the stories.'

'I remember,' replied Alys with a smile. 'I could never get the wings right.' They both laughed. Senni was stretched out on her back, her head cradled in Alys's lap. Alys was idly playing with the curls of her sister's hair, weaving plaits and separating them again. Arkyn and Garran lay on their stomachs in front of the firepit, heads resting on their hands. The four of them stared at the fire's fading embers.

Most families had gone back to their own homes and

their own fires. A few of the older children stayed behind. This was a custom. If you had seen ten winters you were allowed to watch the fire until it had gone out.

'But I don't like it when the norwolf kills the firehawk,' she added.

'That would never really happen,' said Alys. 'A norwolf couldn't jump onto the back of a firehawk. Firehawks are too big, even for a norwolf.'

'Rubbish,' said Garran sharply. 'My father has seen a norwolf jump twenty paces from a standing start. Anyway,' he went on, 'firehawks are not all that big.'

Arkyn groaned. Garran often spoke like this, as if his word was law – a law passed by his father, Dorregan. He expected everyone to listen to him, even if they were older. Alys caught her sister's eye. They smiled at each other. They were used to Garran's ways.

'Your father seems to have seen more norwolves than any hunter alive,' Alys remarked. 'How come he's never actually brought one back on a pole?'

Garran said nothing. Arkyn rolled over onto his side so that his back was turned away from him. He could sense Garran's shame. He didn't want to make things any worse.

Alys had a point though. Garran's father was the latest in

a long line of chiefs from his family. All of them had hunted and killed a norwolf. It was expected. But Dorregan, so far, had failed. And the settlement was close to the Frozen Forest where there were known to be several norwolf packs. Surely that made his failure even worse?

Dorregan's thunderous voice and heavy manner loomed large in Arkyn's imagination. He was an angry man. His failure in the hunt was like a wound that would never heal. The chief was supposed to be the strongest man in the settlement. Yet he had never killed a norwolf. How did Garran feel about that? Arkyn rolled back onto his stomach and looked across at him. Maybe it wasn't so great to be the son of the chief after all.

Arkyn watched Garran staring into the embers, frowning. They never talked about what happened that night in Giant's Cave, even though at least six full moons had passed.

'It's a dumb story anyway,' he declared at last.

Senni raised a sleepy leg and kicked him. 'How can you say that?'

'Because the norwolf attacks the firehawk for no reason. It would never do that. A norwolf would never go after such a dangerous animal. It would hunt cattle or sheep, or maybe wild horses. It would never hunt a firehawk.'

'Maybe if it was hungry enough,' said Alys.

Arkyn didn't reply. Instead, he picked up a thin stick and dragged a lump of glowing wood out of the fire with it. He blew gently on the charred remains until it shone brightly. Small flames licked up around its edges. The wood burned brightly for a few moments, then it faded. He flicked it back into the fire with a sigh.

'I just don't see why everyone hates norwolves so much,' he said at last.

Garran grunted. 'Because they're evil.'

'They're not evil.' Arkyn remembered when Garran had drawn his knife. The pup had looked so fierce, but he was actually terrified. 'They're just animals. People are only afraid because they don't know anything about them.'

'I know that they slaughtered the settlers in the Frozen Forest.'

'Those are just stories, made-up tales to stop children wandering off. The settlers left the Frozen Forest because it was too cold. It wasn't because of the norwolves.'

'You're just upset because your pup has gone,' said Garran. His voice had a mocking tone. 'Should have killed it when we had the chance,' he added.

'Like you would have dared.' Arkyn stared into the fading

fire. He could feel anger building inside him again. Just as it did the night Garran tried to kill the pup.

'There's no point in fighting about it now,' said Alys. 'Arkyn was right about the norwolf. We did a good thing.'

'We did,' agreed Senni. 'And he was always going to leave eventually.'

Arkyn looked across at Garran. Neither of them spoke, but they both had the same thought. Have you told them what really happened that night? Garran was about to say something when a shadow fell across them. They all looked up. It was the storyteller.

***

'Watching the fire fade,' he said, 'is always my favourite part of a story telling. It's often better,' he added with a knowing smile, 'than listening to the story itself.' Arkyn was surprised by the storyteller's gentle manner. He was used to hearing him raise his voice. He could even howl like an animal if the story called for it. Now he seemed almost shy.

'I am sorry if I've disturbed you,' he said. He looked around as he spoke. 'I came to see if I had left something here.'

'What?' said Senni. Then she corrected herself, in case she had sounded rude. 'I mean, can we help you? What are you looking for?'

'My staff,' he replied. 'Quite a long piece of wood. Yew, actually. About this high.' He raised his hand so that it was level with his chest. Of course, they all knew exactly what he was talking about.

'You mean the storypole?' said Alys. Arkyn noticed the anxiety in her voice and he wasn't surprised. He felt it too. The storypole was as much a part of their childhood as the stories themselves. It was difficult to imagine one without the other.

'Well, yes,' he replied quietly, his head bowed. He was obviously embarrassed. 'I'm afraid so. I'm always putting it down in odd places. Then I forget where I've left it.'

'What kind of a storyteller loses his storypole?' mumbled Garran under his breath.

Arkyn shrugged and smiled weakly. He had to admit it was disheartening. The storyteller *he* knew had a voice that could work magic. He could fill the valley with his roar. He could whisper like a tiny mountain stream. He had eyes that saw everything and missed nothing. His arms waved across the sky like clouds of thunder. He had

70

the large hands of a craftsman who could summon bolts of lightning or cast magic spells. When he stood before his audience, telling a story, it felt as if the world itself was speaking.

The man standing before them had the face of the storyteller. But everything else about him seemed wrong. He was no taller than Senni (who was the tallest of the four of them). He stood weakly, with his arms by his sides, his hands hidden in the folds of his cloak, as if he was ashamed of them. His shoulders didn't look broad enough to carry his head. He stood like a willow tree stands over a stream, with a slight lean. Even his cloak looked shabby.

Arkyn stared at him, open-mouthed. Garran was right. What kind of storyteller would lose his storypole?

'Do you remember when you had it last?' said Senni.

The old man's hands appeared from within his cloak. They were small and delicate. 'That's just it,' he said. He turned his hands outwards in a forlorn gesture. 'I can't remember.' He sat down on a nearby rock and closed his eyes. 'Oh dear,' he said. He slouched forward, his head in his hands. 'I hope it hasn't happened again...'

'What do you mean?' said Alys, sitting down next to him. 'What do you hope hasn't happened?'

The storyteller did not reply. He sat with his head in his hands, mumbling to himself.

'Oh come on,' said Garran suddenly, using his son-of-a-chief voice. 'Speak up! You call yourself a storyteller and yet you can't even string a sentence together.'

Arkyn looked at Garran in shock. 'You can't speak to him like that,' he half-whispered. 'He's the storyteller.'

'And he's a guest,' added Alys quickly. 'You know the laws of hosting.'

The old man stopped mumbling and looked up. He was not offended. 'No, it's all right,' he said. 'Your friend is quite right.' He sat up, took a small breath, and looked Garran directly in the eyes.

'Young man,' he said simply, 'I suspect your firehawk has taken it.'

***

The storyteller's words baffled Arkyn. But that was nothing compared to the impact they had on Garran. He stared at the old man as if he had taken leave of his senses. '*My* firehawk?' he said, sounding utterly puzzled. 'What on earth do you mean *my* firehawk?'

'Exactly what I said,' replied the storyteller. 'Your firehawk has flown off with my storypole.' He stared up into the night sky, where countless stars shone brightly, and tutted. 'It's not the first time this has happened. They are ever so difficult to see at night, and fast as lightning.' He pulled himself up onto his feet, sighing heavily. 'It must have been waiting for me as I returned to my shelter…' He turned to Garran and gave him an accusing look. 'Yours is particularly fond of the shiny brass caps.'

'But it's not *my* firehawk,' protested Garran. 'I don't have a firehawk.'

The storyteller stared at him.

'You are Chief Dorregan's son?' he said finally.

'I am,' said Garran. He seemed to raise his chin a little as he spoke.

'Quite so,' said the storyteller with a smile. He placed a hand on Garran's shoulder. It was odd, but the old man appeared to grow taller while he stood there. His voice, too, changed. It was deeper and louder. He was far more like the storyteller they knew.

'Well then, Garran Firebrand,' he said slowly. It was unusual to hear Garran called by his full name. The storyteller continued: 'Son of Dorregan, grandson of Wintergarde…'

Suddenly, there was great strength in his voice. It was a voice that could not be ignored. 'A boy in your high position should know that every settlement has a firehawk nesting close by. It is one of the few things you can be sure about in this uncertain land.'

He looked deeply into Garran's eyes, as if expecting a nod of understanding. But Garran's face was blank. Arkyn, too, was confused. He knew nothing of the habits of firehawks. He glanced at the twins, but even they looked puzzled. Clearly this was something none of them had heard before. He turned back to the storyteller, whose face had grown rather sorrowful. The old man was clearly disappointed by their collective ignorance.

Arkyn felt as if they had all let him down in some way. But how were they to know? They had been raised to view the world beyond the settlement as a place for hunting and foraging only. The animals and plants provided food and shelter, but not much else. It was above all a dangerous and hostile land.

Now he started to wonder. Was there was more to it than that? After all, firehawks nesting near settlements were no stranger than a talking norwolf. Perhaps there was more to this wilderness than endless forests and distant mountains.

'Why would a firehawk nest near a settlement?'

'It has always been this way,' said the storyteller. 'I cannot tell you why, only that it is so.'

Garran's eyes narrowed. 'But why did you say "my" firehawk?'

The storyteller sighed. His voice softened to its former rather weak tone.

'Because your family leads the settlement. The firehawk that nests here will know this. It will know your father, and it will know you. It will be ready to serve you, should you ask for its help.'

Garran looked perplexed. 'But my father said nothing of this.'

The storyteller sighed. He sat down on the rock again. 'Yes, well, it's quite possible that your father has put all this to the back of his mind,' he said sadly. 'He may even have chosen to ignore it. He has always been more interested in hunting.'

Senni sat down next to the storyteller and leaned in close to him. Her eyes were shining with interest. Arkyn heard the tremor of excitement in her voice. 'So… are you saying that a firehawk is nesting near here?'

'I am.'

'Do you know where?'

'Of course,' he said with a slight frown. He shuffled along the stone, away from her. 'I assumed it was well known.' He looked uneasy, as if unsure whether he should tell them. 'But I don't know whether…'

Senni moved in close to him again, her eyes pleading. '*Please* tell us,' she said, fixing him with her widest smile.

'It's been a while since I was up there.' He hesitated. Then he seemed to make a decision. 'But a firehawk rarely moves its nest. It should still be on top of the crags, just above the highest waterfall.'

Senni turned to her friends. Arkyn could see from her eyes what was coming next. 'Shall we go?' she said.

Arkyn and Alys groaned. Garran was silent.

'I… er… I wouldn't advise it, young lady,' said the story-teller quickly.

'Why not?'

'Because if you visit the nest of a firehawk, you run the risk of bumping into the firehawk itself. And they have fearsome tempers.'

'*And* we're ice-bound, Senni. Remember?' said Alys. 'We're not allowed beyond the fence until the river thaws.'

Senni threw up her arms in frustration. 'But it's a *firehawk* nest,' she exclaimed. 'Don't you remember the stories that mother told us? Firehawk nests are full of treasures. Gems as big as your fist.'

'Quite so,' chuckled the storyteller. He smiled at Senni fondly. 'A firehawk's nest is full of surprises.' He turned away and settled his gaze on the fading embers. 'But,' he said in a quiet, serious voice, 'I'm not sure I would be brave enough to go hunting for treasure in such a place.' Arkyn watched as the light from the fire played upon the old man's face, casting dark shadows around his eyes. How quickly the storyteller's mood had changed. Arkyn found himself again wondering how much he really knew about the world beyond the settlement.

Alys stood up, brushing down her leggings as if preparing to leave. 'I am afraid bravery doesn't come into it,' she said. Arkyn noticed the direct look she gave her sister. 'We're *all* ice-bound until the thaw comes.'

***

Next morning, Arkyn woke before dawn. He hadn't slept
well. He had dreamt that a firehawk had landed in the
centre of the settlement and it was breathing spirals of
flame, destroying many huts and shelters. Alys and Senni
were trapped inside one burning hut and they couldn't get
out. He had searched for his father but couldn't find him
anywhere. People were screaming and shouting. Then the
firehawk turned into a norwolf. That was when he woke up.

He rubbed his eyes. A pale dawn light was slowly revealing
the room. He was in Alys and Senni's cabin. The four of
them had slept there after the storytelling. Sleepovers were
common when they were younger, but not so much lately.
The room was familiar, though. A basket full of straw dolls
and wooden animals sat in one corner. A rope ladder lay
coiled in another. Senni's catapult hung from the back of
the door. He briefly wondered where Alys's was. Hers was
a good one. Well-balanced and deadly accurate.

He could hear Tanita moving around in the next room.
The twins' mother was singing softly, a familiar tune. Arkyn
lay still for a moment, listening. It was not a sound he ever
heard in his own shelter. He pictured her moving swiftly

about the room, attending to chores and preparing for the day. She was a small, slight woman with delicate features and a gentle manner. Gentle until she encountered an injustice, that is. You could always rely on Tanita to speak up if she believed a wrong had been done. It was a quality her daughters had inherited.

The outer door opened and closed with a soft clack. The singing disappeared down the alley, muffled by the snow. She visited the settlement elders most days, suggesting remedies if they were sick or just checking up on them.

Arkyn looked across to where Senni and Alys had thrown blankets and furs onto the wooden floorboards, making themselves a temporary bed. He could see Alys's black hair poking out from beneath a large woollen throw. There was something odd about Senni, though. The lump under her blanket was a strange shape. He watched it for a few moments, waiting for the rise and fall of her breath. Nothing. He kicked back his own blanket and crawled across the boards on his knees. He gave the lump a nudge. Then a firmer prod. He pulled back the cover and saw a pillow and a bundle of clothes.

An icy breeze blew in from a small window at the back of the room. Arkyn shivered. Who would leave a window open during this season? The river was frozen solid. The snow was knee deep. He stood up, meaning to close it. Then he stopped and looked again at Senni's pillow and clothes. Next to her pillow was a tiny straw model. A firehawk. A terrible thought dawned on him.

He leaned across and gave Alys's shoulder a shove. 'Alys,' he whispered. 'Wake up.' He looked across to where Garran lay sleeping. His face was mostly hidden beneath a pile of furs but Arkyn could see his eyes were closed. When he turned back to Alys she was awake and alert, her dark brown eyes staring at him. 'What?' she said.

'Senni's gone,' he whispered.

'She's probably gone out with mother.'

'I don't think so. Your mother's only just left and I'm certain Senni wasn't with her.'

Alys propped herself up on one elbow. She scratched her head and yawned.

'And look at this.' He showed her the way Senni's pillow and clothes had been shaped to look like a body. 'I think she wanted to slip out without anyone noticing.' Alys studied the space where Senni had slept. 'And there's also this,' he added, handing over the straw firehawk.

Arkyn watched her eyes widen as she took the small

model. 'Oh no,' she said at last, no longer whispering. 'You don't think?'

'I don't know,' he said, keeping his voice down. 'But I reckon we shouldn't wake Garran.'

Alys glanced across the room. She sat up fully, crossing her legs and wrapping a blanket around her body. She took the firehawk and turned it over in her fingers. 'She hasn't made one of these for ages.'

'You heard her last night,' said Arkyn. 'She was desperate to go and look for the firehawk nest. I bet she's gone on her own.'

'Blood and blades.' Alys reached for her boots and began to pull them on. 'Of all the stupid things... I knew I shouldn't have told her not to go there, it has just encouraged her.'

Arkyn said nothing, but he could guess what was coming. If Senni had gone looking for the firehawk's nest then they would have to go after her. It was too dangerous to be out in the forest on your own. Not to mention the cold. Or the trouble she would be in if someone found out.

He watched as Alys wrapped long lengths of woollen cloth around her ankles to keep out the snow. He looked around the room, wondering where his own boots had gone. He finally spotted them under Garran's blanket and pulled them free with a careful tug. Apart from boots and coats there wasn't much more dressing to be done. It was always this way when the snow came. Everyone slept in their clothes.

Fresh snow had fallen in the night. It was only just getting light and there were few footprints on the ground. They spotted traces of Senni's steps straight away. Tanita's prints were also there, leading towards the centre of the settlement. Senni's, on the other hand, went around the back of the hut.

She was clearly heading for the narrow gate at the far end of the settlement, where she was less likely to be seen.

***

They followed Senni's tracks as far as the gate. After that it got much harder. Everything was white, both in the sky and on the ground. The light was dazzling. Footprints were almost impossible to see. Even the usual path leading away from the settlement was hidden.

Arkyn stuggled to keep up with Alys. He was amazed how swiftly she could follow Senni's footprints, as if she knew exactly the route she would take. Was it because they were twins? He pictured them joined by an invisible thread, one forever following the other.

He glanced back every few minutes to check that no one had seen them. The narrow gate had been bolted but there was no one around. It had been simple enough to slip through the gap in the fence they often used. Senni had most likely gone the same way.

'How long do we have?' he said.

'Just the morning, at most,' replied Alys. 'Mother won't suspect anything if we miss the morning meal. But she will start to worry if we are not at home by the middle of the day.'

'My father will probably sleep until then anyway.' Now that he thought about it, he hadn't seen his father since the previous morning. Not that that was unusual. They didn't spend a lot of time together.

'We still need to get a move on. Senni can't be that much further ahead.'

Arkyn stopped suddenly.

'What's wrong?' asked Alys.

'I was just thinking about Garran.'

'What about him?'

'I was wondering what he'll do when he wakes up and finds we've gone.'

'He'll probably just go home.' Alys sniffed and set off again, lifting her knees high through the thick snow.

Arkyn stared after her, unconvinced that things would turn out that simply. He was starting to wonder whether they were making a big mistake. 'What if he sees your mother?' he shouted after her. 'They'll soon start to wonder where we've gone.'

'There's no point in worrying about that now. Let's just get on with finding Senni.'

Arkyn took several running strides through the snow. 'We should have told him where we were going,' he said, panting heavily as he caught up with her.

'Why? So he could tell his father?'

'He wouldn't do that.'

'Of course he would. You remember what he was like about the norwolf? I can just imagine him now.' She stopped for a moment, puffing out her chest and tilting her head back. Then she mimicked Garran's voice. 'I am the chief's son,' she barked. 'My father should know.'

Arkyn grinned. Maybe she was right. He could feel the confusion in his heart, though. Garran and he were practically brothers. But he *had* tried to kill the norwolf pup. 'Yeah, maybe,' he said at last.

Alys shrugged and walked on. 'Come on. It's too late to go back now anyway. We'll just have to hope that he's stuck inside doing chores. He'll never think that we've actually left the settlement.'

Arkyn nodded. It's true, he thought. You'd be mad to come out in this weather.

There was a light snowfall, but no wind. Thick flakes were settling easily. Further away from the settlement the path rose steadily and steeply. The bare earth was frozen solid, with patches of sheet ice in places. The climb was slippery and dangerous. Fresh snow fell on the ice, settling quickly. After a while the path grew too icy. It was impossible to climb up any more. Arkyn slipped, then grabbed a nearby branch to steady himself.

'She can't have come up here,' he gasped.

'But this is the quickest way to the river.'

'Maybe we've got it all wrong. Maybe she's back at your house, wondering where we are.'

'I don't think so… Look!' Alys pointed to a dark brown object on the side of the path. It was one of Senni's mittens. Alys looked at him in triumph. '*Now* do you believe me? She must have stopped here for a moment. Typical of her to lose a glove… And there are more prints over there.'

Alys was right. Senni had stopped trying to climb the icy path. Instead, the tracks led away from the path and into thicker snow among the trees. Now there was more grip, and Alys and Arkyn reached the top of the climb quickly. From there they had a clear view of the river. Arkyn stood with his mouth open, astonished. He knew that the water was frozen, but he didn't expect it to look like this. It was as if nature itself had been brought to a stop. The chattering, bubbling current had been stilled. The shape of the river followed the path they had always known, but now it was silent and still. It lay on the valley floor like a dead snake, black and lifeless.

'Wow,' said Alys.

'Yeah,' agreed Arkyn.

Alys had cupped her hands over her eyes, trying to block out the white glare bouncing off the snow. 'It's hard to see far... Can you even see the river crossing?'

Arkyn lifted his hands to his eyes. The snow was falling much more heavily now. 'Only just,' he said. It was a long way. He felt a nervous twitch in the pit of his stomach. This is madness, he thought. Even if they got as far as the crossing stones, they still needed to cross the river. And then they would have to walk upstream to the waterfalls. It was usually a day's walk to the top of the waterfalls and back. And that was in *good* weather. Surely Senni wouldn't go so far on her own, in weather like this?

He wanted to tell Alys that this was all too risky. If Senni was out there, then they needed to go back to the settlement and tell her mother. They had to get more help.

Arkyn opened his mouth to speak.

'There she is!' Alys cried.

***

Arkyn stared into the distance. He couldn't see anything. It was too white. 'Where?'

'Over there! On the other side of the river.'

Arkyn looked again. He could only just make out the shapes of the stones that marked the river crossing. They rose up out of the frozen river like monsters, covered in a thin white coat of snow. He searched the far bank for signs of life. 'I can't see anything,' he said at last.

'You're not looking properly.' She took his arm and aimed it towards a clump of trees close to the edge of the river.

'Over there,' she said. 'See that dark shape below the trees? It's moving.'

Arkyn felt a strange mix of frustration and fear. This was so stupid, he thought. No one should be out in this weather. But he knew that Alys wouldn't give up. She never did. He looked again, squinting into the whiteness. Then he took a breath. There *was* something there. It was climbing up into the trees, away from the river.

'What makes you think that's Senni? It could just be an animal.'

'It's definitely her. I'm sure of it.'

They stood for a moment, staring into the white space. The shape was moving very slowly through the heavy snow. Definitely more human than animal. If it was Senni, then she was heading the right way for the waterfalls.

'Senni!' Alys shouted. She waved her arms in the air, shouting again. 'Senni!'

Arkyn joined in. He still wasn't sure it was her, but it helped him keep warm. They waved their arms madly and screamed until they were hoarse and their throats hurt.

If there had been no wind then their voices would have cut through the silence of the snow with ease. Senni would have heard them straight away. She would have waved and waited for them to catch her up. But the wind was getting stronger and there was no shelter at the top of the hill.

Their cries were picked up and dragged down the valley, away from Senni's ears. The figure kept moving towards the trees. Then it was gone, into the darkness of the wood and out of sight.

'Come on,' said Alys quickly. 'Let's get after her.'

Arkyn hesitated. 'Are you sure? Maybe we should get help?'

Alys's nostrils flared with anger. 'You're joking, right?'

'But look at the sky. The storm's getting worse. No one should be out in this. It's too dangerous.'

'We can't *leave* her!'

'I don't mean leave her. I just mean we should get help. Go back and tell your mother, or even my father. They'll know what to do.' Arkyn paused when he thought about his father. Maybe it wouldn't be a great idea to tell him after all. He would just tell them it was too bad. He'd say something about kids needing to learn. If Senni was stupid enough to go out in this weather then... Arkyn felt a knot of anger rising in his belly. He had started to notice that feeling whenever he thought about his father. It had become a familiar sensation, like an itch that wouldn't go away. Maybe, he decided, he should just show his father that he could look after himself. That he didn't need anyone else's help. Maybe Alys was right. Maybe they could rescue Senni by themselves.

Alys had already set off down the hill towards the frozen river. 'You do what you like,' she called back, 'I'm going after her.'

Arkyn looked up. Bulging white clouds, heavy with snow, gathered slowly above them. 'Wait,' he shouted, 'I'm coming.'

She paused, waiting for Arkyn to catch up. 'I knew you'd come around,' she said with a grin. 'Come on. We can move much faster than she can. We'll catch her in no time.'

'Yeah? And when we've caught her... what are we going to do then?' Arkyn knew that when Senni put her mind to it she was like a hound on the scent of blood.

'Well, I don't know about you,' she said, 'but I'm going to give her a kicking.'

***

Crossing the frozen river was easier than Arkyn expected. The rocks were slippery but the wind was not as strong as it had been on the hill. He was pleased with his footwork over the stones. Not quite as quick as Alys, perhaps, but his long legs and taller frame worked against him. Alys could keep her body low, and she hardly ever lost her balance. Arkyn allowed himself a quiet victory cry as he leapt from the final stone onto the bank. A few stamps into the snow proved he was on solid ground again. That was a comfort. When he looked up Alys had already set off along the riverbank. Clearly they were not taking any more breaks. He took a deep breath and ploughed on.

They followed the edge of the forest as it traced the path of the river, heading upstream towards the waterfalls. The water was not frozen up here. Its slow current ran like a cold, syrupy shiver through the valley. The surface of the water was almost black. Arkyn shuddered as they raced on. It would not be good to fall in there.

Still there was no sign of Senni. They ran whenever the pathway was clear enough to do so. The rest of the time they marched, like the hunters did when there were long distances to cover. Eventually they reached the top of the crags. This was the highest point of the climb. They could hear the four waterfalls roaring nearby, although they couldn't actually see them. If the storyteller was right, then the firehawk's nest was near.

They stopped in a small clearing. 'I don't understand,' said Alys, scanning the woodland for signs of life, 'we should have caught up with her by now.' Arkyn slumped down onto a fallen tree trunk. He was exhausted. He felt he should offer a word of comfort, but he couldn't think of any. The gentle rumbling in his stomach told him that it must be past the middle of the day. How late was it, he wondered? He scanned the sky, searching for the position of the sun, but it was impossible to find. There was just white wintry light, stretched evenly over their heads like a veil. The journey of the day was impossible to measure.

'Senni!' he shouted. It was a desperate call, the loudest he could summon. He wasn't really sure what else to do.

'Over here!' came a cry.

Alys and Arkyn looked at each other in shock. Surely not? Alys's eyes brightened hopefully. 'Senni,' she cried. 'Where are you? Call again!'

'It came from over there,' said Arkyn. 'Behind those trees.'

There was a cluster of beech trees about fifty paces away. From a distance, they looked like part of the woods. But as Alys and Arkyn got closer they realised there was something unusual about them. They had grown in a perfect circle.

'Up here,' came a shout.

They stepped into the circle of trees and looked up. A vast net of branches weaved above them. Each limb had grown across the next, some under and some over. The effect was of a giant wooden web. Arkyn stared in wonder, he had never seen anything like it before.

A familiar voice called down: 'Coo-ee!'

Senni had climbed up to the first layer of branches. Her cheeks were red and rosy. Her eyes were bright. She looked very pleased with herself.

'Senni!' shouted Alys. 'Are you mad? You're gonna get us in such trouble!'

Senni's legs swung playfully beneath the branches. 'Come on… don't be pathetic. Nobody will have missed us yet.' She peered over the branches into the wooden web. There was a shrill cry of delight. 'You *must* come and see this. It's amazing!'

Arkyn was about to start climbing up, but he hesitated when he noticed Alys hadn't moved. He looked up at Senni.

'Have you seen the weather?' he asked. 'It's getting worse, and there isn't much light left.'

Senni glared down at him. 'Arkyn, it's not like you to be so dreary.'

Arkyn felt himself blushing in silent fury.

'*Come* on…' She softened her voice. 'We've still got plenty of time. You've got to see this. I think it's the firehawk's nest.'

Senni was right. It *was* the firehawk's nest. Arkyn was surprised. He had thought it would be in a cave or a hollow of some kind. An adult firehawk was said to have a wingspan of over fifty paces. Surely they didn't build nests like normal birds? But here it was. A nest. A very large and complex nest. The branches had been carefully placed between the boughs of the trees to form a sort of net. Large, sturdy limbs took most of the weight, with smaller ones threaded in between. The branches had been covered in ferns and leaves. It was like a normal bird's nest. Just much, much bigger.

'Incredible, isn't it?' said Senni, as Alys and then Arkyn climbed up to join her. All three peered over the edge.

'It looks quite comfortable,' said Arkyn.

'And warm,' agreed Alys.

Arkyn spotted something purple poking out from beneath the leaves at the centre of the nest. Some kind of cloth or item of clothing. 'What's that?'

'Looks like a scarf,' said Senni.

'I know what that is,' said Alys. 'It's the storyteller's. He ties it to the storypole.'

'Then he was right,' said Senni. 'The firehawk did take the storypole. We need to get it back for him.'

'No we don't,' said Alys firmly. 'We need to go now. We've been here too long as it is.'

'It won't take me a second,' said Senni. 'If the nest is strong enough for a firehawk then it's definitely strong enough for me.'

'Wait Senni!' Alys reached out to grab her sister's arm, but she was too late. Senni clambered over the edge of the nest and began to climb down into the centre. Arkyn tightened his grip on the branch he was sitting on. He had a strong feeling that this was not going to end well.

'You're impossible!' Alys thumped a nearby branch with the palm of her hand. 'Why don't you just listen for once?'

'Calm down. I've got it. I'm coming back now.' Senni was tugging at the scarf. They could see the tip of the storypole, but she was struggling to pull it free.

'It's stuck fast,' she said. She pulled harder, but the stick wouldn't budge.

Arkyn shivered and looked up into the sky. The wind pressed against his face, growing in force. The clouds seemed darker. There was a strange mood in the air. 'Hang on Senni,' he called. 'I think you should stop… come back.'

Senni wasn't listening. She was digging away in the middle of the nest, trying to release the storypole

'It's coming,' she said. She kept pulling. The stick was moving, but only slowly. Alys started to climb down into the nest too. Arkyn put his arm out and stopped her.

'What's up?' she said.

'I'm not sure. I just feel like something's wrong.' He turned away from the nest and looked back into the thick of the woods. What was that noise? It wasn't the waterfalls. It was something else. It was like the sound he had heard when he first saw the norwolf pup. But it was different. It was colder. Sharper.

Slowly, he started to understand what it was. It was a shriek, a distant scream. And it was getting louder.

'Senni!' He heard the crack in his voice as he shouted at her. 'Leave it.' He could feel his fear right down to his toes. 'Get back here. We've got to get down and hide.' But he already knew they were too late. The shadow fell upon them like night itself. It was the firehawk.

***

The giant bird hovered above the treetops, each massive beat of its broad wings sending a wave of cold air down over them. The firehawk's huge black eyes were shining with fury. Senni screamed and crouched down as low as she could, curling herself up into a ball.

The firehawk shrieked back, a thousand times louder. Its terrible cry ripped through the trees. Arkyn and Alys braced themselves against the side of the nest and covered their ears with their hands.

'Senni,' cried Alys. 'Get over here!'

Alys edged deeper into the nest, getting as close as she could to her sister. It was hard, though. The firehawk's wings were causing chaos. Branches were bending and flexing. Leaves and sticks were thrown everywhere. Arkyn gripped Alys's hand as she leaned across. She shouted to her sister. 'Take my arm!'

Senni reached out. But she didn't let go of the storypole. To her horror, Alys realised that she was still trying to pull it out of the nest.

'Just leave it,' she cried. 'It doesn't matter.'

'It's coming,' Senni insisted. 'Just one more pull…'

The pole came free with a sudden jolt, pitching Senni onto her side. She lost her grip on Alys and fell into the belly of the nest with the pole in her hand. The shrieks of the firehawk grew louder. It was as if the sight of the storypole had enraged it even more. Arkyn, watching from the side, suddenly understood why.

The nest was moving. It was rocking from side to side. The longest and thickest branches across the middle began to sway backwards and forwards. Moving the pole had weakened it in some way, and now the whole structure was untying itself.

It happened so fast there was no time to save Senni. Huge gaps appeared in the frame of the nest. The main wooden limbs that had seemed so strong, fell aside like tiny sticks. Arkyn focused all his efforts on hanging on to Alys. She screamed in fright as the nest gave way, the whole structure crashing down, taking Senni with it.

'Hold on!' he shouted.

Alys gripped tightly but her eyes were wild with panic. She managed to clamber up to join him, then turned back to where the nest had been. 'Senni!' she yelled.

Senni made no sound as she fell, but they saw she was still holding the storypole.

There was an awful, wood-splitting crash as the nest hit the ground. The firehawk, and the whole forest, fell silent. Even the roar of the waterfalls seemed to stop. The only sound was the slow, heavy beat of the firehawk's wings. Then, from the horrified creature, a cry of anguish.

Arkyn and Alys clung to each other in the cradle of the tree. Just in front of them was a huge space where the nest had been. Arkyn stared straight into that empty space, hardly believing what had just happened.

***

The firehawk spotted the two children stranded in the tree. Arkyn felt his stomach lurch. He was sure it was looking straight at them. Then it turned its head to the sky. Its wing beats quickened. Swells of air drummed down upon the tops of the trees with growing speed as the giant bird soared upwards.

Arkyn was surprised by how easily the firehawk moved, given its enormous size. It opened its wings wide. The feathers were the colour of a roaring fire flecked with shining specks of gold. The effect was dazzling, like something out of a dream. The beak, on the other hand, was from a nightmare. It was chipped and scarred. Arkyn guessed they were battle scars.

The firehawk rose upwards until it was in clear air. Then it began to circle above them. Once, twice, three times. Each time it flew faster and faster until, at the end of the fourth circle, it opened its beak wide. Arkyn expected to hear the awful, deafening scream. But no sound came. Instead he watched, open-mouthed, as a thick spray of flame burst from the firehawk's beak. The fire ripped through the air as if an army of demons had been let loose, setting the sky alight.

Alys had turned pale and she was breathing hard. Her woollen leggings were torn. Red marks ran down her leg where she had been scratched by splinters of wood.

She looked at Arkyn. 'Any ideas?'

'Let's keep still,' he said. 'Maybe it's just showing its anger. Maybe it will fly away.'

'It's not going to fly away. It blames us.'

'Well, *we* can't run away, can we? Even if we could get out of this tree it would catch us in a moment.'

Alys bent forward and looked down. 'Can you see Senni?'

'No…' he replied. 'Actually, I don't know.' Arkyn's back was pressed firmly against the solid trunk of the tree. He felt safer that way. 'I haven't looked.'

Alys made a sudden choking sound, like a sob. 'What if she's dead?'

'She'll be all right. It's not that far down. I expect the branches broke her fall.'

'Then why hasn't she called out?'

Arkyn had no answer to that.

There was no more time to look for Senni. The fire-hawk was dropping down towards them once more. This time, however, it thrust its claws forward and settled easily on the crown of a tall tree near them. Until that moment, Arkyn had not really noticed the claws. In spite of being scared out of his wits, he was enthralled. The bird was as big as his home, and yet it was also light enough to balance with the grace of a small bird.

Without warning, an image of the norwolf pup flashed through his mind. Strangely, though, the pup was no longer a pup. He was almost fully grown. His fur was as white as the landscape around them. The dark colouring around his nose and mouth had got blacker.

Arkyn's ears were ringing. Just as they had done before. This time, though, he welcomed the sounds. Had the nor-wolf been there all the time? Had he been watching them?

Arkyn hadn't tried talking in his head since he had parted

from the norwolf in the cave. It was such a difficult thing to do. All his other thoughts just seemed to get in the way. But they were in real danger now. He felt he had no choice but to try.

Are you here? he began. He noticed that his silent voice was almost pleading. *If you are, please help us!*

Then he saw him. A silent shape framed against the snow: the norwolf, standing on the far side of the fallen nest.

As if in answer, he raised his head and howled. It was a long, haunting howl, like a battle cry. Then he lowered his entire body to snarl at the firehawk. His lips rolled back, baring bright white teeth.

Arkyn wondered if it was possible for a firehawk to look startled. How dare you? it seemed to say. But there was a flicker of fear in those dark eyes too. Alys gripped Arkyn's arm tightly. 'Arkyn,' she whispered. 'Please tell me that's the norwolf we helped.'

'It is,' he said.

'But it hasn't even been a whole winter. He's massive!'

'Don't worry. He won't hurt us.'

'How can you be sure?'

'Because he's come to help us.'

She looked at him. 'What are you talking about?'

Arkyn wasn't sure how much more to say. 'Just trust me,' he said. 'I think it's going to be OK.'

The firehawk was calling out with shrill, short squawks. But its call was not as loud as before. The norwolf seemed to grow as the fur along his back rose up. He took a step forward, still snarling. The firehawk gave one last, irate cry, then it launched into the air. Within a breath, it was above the treetops. There was another desperate cry. Then it flew away.

The norwolf stopped snarling. He sat down on his haunches and looked up at them.

Quick. Your friend needs you.

***

Senni was lying under a pile of ferns. She was still holding the storypole. She was alive, but she had landed badly on her ankle.

'The bone could be broken,' said Alys. 'Can you put any weight on it?'

Senni's face was pale. She looked cold. 'I think so,' she said. Arkyn and Alys took an arm each and helped her up.

She tried to put some weight on her foot, but screamed

with pain. 'No,' she gasped. 'I can't. I'm sorry. It hurts too much.'

They laid her down on the ground again. Arkyn found himself turning to the norwolf for help, thinking that he would know what to do. He was even on the verge of speaking out loud but stopped himself just in time.

Senni shuddered. 'I'm freezing,' she said.

Alys took off her fleece and wrapped it around her sister's shoulders. She looked up at the trees. The light was fading. 'The sun's going down,' she said. 'That's why you're getting colder.'

She looked worried. 'Now we're in trouble.'

'And we weren't before?'

'How are we going to get her back to the settlement? We can't carry her and if we stay here much longer she's going to freeze. We all are.'

The norwolf took a step towards Arkyn, so that the ridge of his back was alongside him. It was a shock to see him so close. He was so big, bigger than any wolf he had ever seen. Almost the size of a small horse, but Arkyn felt no fear. Quite the opposite, he felt safer than he had ever felt before.

Use the nest, thought the norwolf.

What do you mean?

Use the leaves to keep warm. Build shelter.

'Oh I see,' Arkyn said out loud. 'Of course!'

Alys looked at him with a puzzled expression. 'Who are you talking to?'

'Nobody,' he said quickly. He felt his cheeks flushing. 'I was just thinking out loud. We could use these branches and ferns to make a shelter. We can even make a fire.'

Alys looked around uncertainly. 'I think we should try to get back now. We can't spend the night out here.'

Arkyn took the end of a long branch. He wedged one end into the elbow of a nearby tree. Then he started laying other branches against that one.'I don't think we have a choice. Our only hope is to build a camp and wait for help. They'll come looking for us, I'm sure of it.'

Alys stood watching for a moment. Then she started gathering fern fronds off the floor.

Senni shivered and groaned. 'I'm so cold,' she moaned.

The norwolf padded over to her. He seemed to study her tiny body. Arkyn and Alys stopped working for a moment and watched. Alys look horrified.

'Hey,' said Alys. 'What's he doing?'

'Don't worry,' said Arkyn. 'He won't hurt her.'

The norwolf lay down next to the shivering girl. He pushed his massive body right up against her. Senni was rigid with shock for a moment. Then, slowly, she leaned into the animal's fur and sighed. 'Mmm, that's so warm.' She smiled weakly and closed her eyes. The norwolf laid his head across her stomach. His long, thick neck gave extra warmth on top of her body. Then the great beast looked at Arkyn.

Hurry, he thought. *She'll be all right for now, but you need a shelter and a fire.*

Arkyn nodded. He turned back to his task.

Alys stared at the norwolf in wonder, her mouth half open.

'I can hardly believe what I'm seeing.'

'I told you,' said Arkyn. 'Norwolves aren't all bad.'

***

The shelter was built quickly. The firehawk's nest was full of sticks and branches that they could use. There were piles of leaves, soft moss and fern fronds too.

'We could have made a dozen dens,' laughed Arkyn. He kicked one side of the shelter with his boot, just to check it was stable. A solid job, he decided. It had been hard work, but his whole body felt warm. He looked over at Senni and the norwolf. They had moved her into the shelter and the norwolf had curled up next to her again. She was fast asleep.

Snow had been falling steadily all evening. The waterfalls still raged in the distance, but the forest itself was quiet.

Alys had built a long, narrow fire along the open side of the den. It was a trick the girls had been shown by their mother. It was quick to put out and it gave off heat all across the shelter. Now she was lying on the other side of her sister, helping the norwolf keep her warm.

Arkyn smiled to himself. This was good. They were under cover. They were warm. They had a norwolf as guard. Nothing could touch them out here. The norwolf seemed to be asleep, but every now and then he would open his large eyes and stare out into the woods. Arkyn had no idea what he was looking at. He seemed to see further than any of them, to see deep into the darkness. Beyond it, even. It was as if he could sense things that no one else could.

Arkyn had never forgotten that time in the cave when he had nursed the young pup through his injury. How long had it been? A whole season had passed, from the middle of summer right through to the end of harvest. Now, with the river frozen and snow on the ground, winter was at its deepest. The sun had risen many times since that night in Giant's Cave. What had the norwolf been doing all that time? Had he travelled far? Had he found other norwolves?

You do know that I can hear you?

Arkyn almost jumped out of his skin in shock. The norwolf was watching him closely. Arkyn could have sworn he saw humour in those eyes.

I forgot, Arkyn replied silently. *It's been so long.* He waited for a moment. Then he decided to say what was on his mind. *You've got so big.*

That's how it is, thought the norwolf. *I wouldn't have survived otherwise.*

But you seem… older. I mean, you talk differently.

Do I?

I just remember that… This was all new. The talking, I mean.

It was new to both of us, as I recall.

It still is, to me. Arkyn looked down at the fire. *But you seem better at it now.*

I have been practising.

Arkyn looked up, confused. *What do you mean?*

They call it 'communicating', actually.

I don't understand. Who does? Who have you been talking to?

There are people like you in the place you call the Frozen Forest.

They can talk to you like I can? Arkyn's mind was racing.

They don't only talk to me. They communicate with all kinds of creatures… But in just the same way.

Arkyn was silent. He didn't know what to think. Part of him was excited. If there were others who did this, then maybe it wasn't so strange after all. Maybe there *wasn't* anything wrong with him. But there was another feeling too. It was an angry feeling. He didn't like to think that other people had been talking to 'his' norwolf.

You saved me, thought the norwolf. He seemed to have sensed Arkyn's unease. *I will never forget that.*

And you've saved us now. I won't forget that either.

There is a bond between us, then.

Like brothers in a pack?

Yes, exactly like that.

Arkyn leaned across to touch the norwolf's head. A cold shiver ran through his spine. He shuddered. *What was that?*

Hunters, replied the norwolf. He raised his head. *They are still some distance away, but I must go now. It will be your people. You will be safe now.*

But I can't hear anything. I can't even hear the hunting dogs.

You sensed them though.

I am not sure I did. I just felt cold.

It's a start. You will sense more as you get older.

I don't understand.

You don't need to. You don't need to do anything. The norwolf got up gently, taking care not to disturb Senni and Alys.

When will I see you again? asked Arkyn. He could feel the sorrow swelling within him, rising in his throat. He didn't want to be saying goodbye after such a short time.

I don't know, thought the norwolf. *Soon, I hope.*

His giant paws stepped easily over the sleeping figures of Alys and Senni. He stopped at the edge of the shelter and sniffed the cold air. Arkyn wondered if he was listening for something. The norwolf looked at Arkyn one more time, then turned and loped off into the darkness.

In the distance, a dog barked. Then another. The hunters were coming. Arkyn sighed with relief, feeling his muscles relax properly for the first time since he and Alys had left the settlement. Now they could get Senni home. Now they were safe.

But the sense of sorrow lingered, like a tiny flame that wouldn't go out. He realised that part of him had wanted to go with the norwolf. He wanted to join his pack brother in the heart of the forest. He stared into the darkness, won-. dering which way the animal had gone. Then he smiled to himself. Idiot, he thought. You're no norwolf.

***

It was a grim ride back to the settlement. Arkyn had to share a horse with Garran, who insisted on sitting in front and was angry. Garran had wasted no time in informing Arkyn and Alys that his father Dorregan had wanted to put off the search until at least the next day. He wanted to 'teach the young brats a lesson', according to Garran. Arkyn suspected that Garran agreed with him. It was only Garran's mother who saved the day, insisting they start the search immediately.

Arkyn briefly wondered why Hanserik, his own father, hadn't come with the search party. Perhaps it was not such a surprise. Hanserik tended to leave Arkyn to work things out for himself. He wondered what he would say if he knew about the norwolf. Not that he was going to tell him. Arkyn hadn't said a word about the rescue and he didn't want to make things worse now. Perhaps, he reflected, it would have been different if his mother was still alive.

Senni had been given some herbs to ease the pain. The brew made her talk even more than normal. As Dorregan's men lifted her onto a sled, she said something to them about being 'saved by a norwolf'.

Arkyn shot a nervous glance at Alys, who was perched on the sled next to Senni. He didn't want any of them to say what had happened, about what the norwolf had done. He felt panic rising in his chest. If only they had been able to talk things through before Dorregan and his men had turned up. But he need not have worried. Alys hesitated for the briefest of moments, then calmly explained that Senni had knocked her head when she fell from the nest, and that she had been asleep in the shelter most of the time. 'The norwolf must have been a dream,' she said.

'At least we can give the storyteller his pole back,' continued Senni in the same drowsy voice. 'It'll make it all worth it, even if we do end up doing extra chores for the rest of the winter.' She was still clutching the yew staff. The purple scarf was hanging off the end of it like a wet rag.

'You'll be doing more than a few extra chores,' growled Dorregan. 'At least, you will if I have anything to say about it.' His thick black beard hid so much of his face that Arkyn often found it difficult to judge his mood. His cheeks were always bright red and his eyebrows seemed locked in a permanent scowl. It was the teeth, Arkyn thought. If you could see his teeth then you knew he was *really* angry.

Just then, one of the hunting hounds picked up a scent. It was the lead dog, Claw, a tall, rangy animal with a long, pointed muzzle and a short, glossy black coat bulging with muscle tone. Arkyn reckoned Claw was as swift as any creature in the forest. Now he was mad with excitement, straining at his lead, desperate to chase.

Claw's handler was a young, shaven-headed hunter called Niklas. He was a cheerful man with laughing eyes who was always happy to talk to Arkyn, particularly if the topic was hunting. Niklas had raised Claw from a puppy and loved him with all his heart. Arkyn reckoned he knew that dog better than his own family.

'Control that hound!' Dorregan shouted.

'I'm trying,' gasped Niklas. 'He never behaves like this. Unless…'

'Unless what?' barked Dorregan. 'What does he smell?'

'Unless it's a norwolf, Chief Dorregan.'

Dorregan's eyes grew wide. In the half-light Arkyn watched the big man's face break slowly into a broad grin. Arkyn felt his stomach turn, as if something awful was about to unfold.

'Are you sure, Niklas?'

Arkyn stared at the young hunter, willing him to say no. Maybe it was something else. An ordinary wolf, perhaps. He could tell that Niklas wasn't certain. He was kneeling next to the hound, looking into his eyes. It almost seemed as if he were whispering to him. Arkyn watched closely, strangely fascinated. Is this what it looked like, perhaps, when he spoke to the norwolf? There were no sounds in his head, though, and he knew in his heart that this was not the same. Niklas was master, and Claw knew only one skill: to follow a scent and to kill. It was very different.

Niklas stood up at last. 'I'm sure,' he said to Dorregan. 'It's a norwolf.'

Dorregan turned to Garran, beaming with delight.

'Hear that, boy? Perhaps this search in the freezing night was not such a waste of time after all.' He brought his horse to a stop and issued a flurry of orders. 'Niklas, you stay here for the night. Keep your hound within scent of the beast, but no closer. I will take these imps home and return at first light.'

Arkyn's body turned weak as he listened to Dorregan. Garran leaned back in his horse. He whispered into Arkyn's ear. 'I don't suppose you know anything about this, do you Arkyn? A norwolf lost in these woods… helping children in danger, perhaps?'

Arkyn said nothing. There was nothing to say. There was nothing he could do. Not yet, anyway. But he would do something. He *had* to. He and the norwolf were brothers, after all.

Part 3

Hunt

The howl of the hunting dogs kept Arkyn awake. He muttered a curse and turned over yet again, burying his face in the thin mattress. How long had they been at it? They had started just after nightfall, as soon as the moon appeared over the top of the trees. That felt like hours ago.

At the beginning, Arkyn had recognised the long, haunting howl of Claw. His call had carried across the tops of the trees from the heart of the forest, where he and Niklas had remained. The hunting dogs on the settlement, locked up in kennels, had heard Claw and quickly joined in. It wasn't long before there was a full chorus. Since then, there hadn't been a moment of peace. Arkyn stared at his wall and sighed. Narrow beams of light crept through the gaps. They created strange shadows on the floor. He was surprised no one had shut the dogs up. But then he remembered that it was always this way before a big hunt. The men spent the night in their shelters, sharpening arrowheads. The dogs were left to howl. It was a good omen, people said. It would bring luck to the hunt.

There was a loud knock on his bedroom wall. It was coming from outside the shelter.

'Arkyn, wake up!' shouted Garran. Then more knocking. Each new bang brought an icy shower of snow through the loose slats at the top of the wall.

'Arkyn!' Garran yelled again. He sounded desperate. 'Come on, wake up!'

'What do you want?' Arkyn groaned. He felt as if he had barely closed his eyes. Surely it wasn't morning already?

'We have to get ready! The hunt will be leaving soon!'

Arkyn propped himself up on his elbows. In the wall at the end of his bed there was a small hatch. It was just wide enough for him to crawl through. He had cut it out the previous summer, mainly so that he could get out of the shelter without anyone knowing. The only other way was through the room where his father slept. Arkyn didn't like to disturb his father.

He leaned forward and slid the hatch open. He was greeted by a wall of white snow.

'Where are you?' Garran said. 'The snow's fresh and I can't find the hatch.'

Arkyn punched a fist through the snowed-up hole. Unfortunately, Garran was right there. At least his stomach was. 'Ouch!' He doubled over in pain and surprise. 'What did you do that for?!'

'Sorry,' said Arkyn. 'I didn't know you were so close.' He peered through the small hole. 'Where are you now?'

'Here!' Garran replied. He kicked the remains of the snow into Arkyn's room – and onto his bed – with his boot. 'Now we're even.'

'Idiot!' shouted Arkyn. He quickly dusted the snow off his clothes and rug, knowing how long they would take to dry if he didn't. He turned back to the open hatch. Cold air was pouring into the room like an icy cough. Arkyn shuddered as he sat on his bed. Slowly, his eyes adjusted to the bright light.

'Come on,' Garran repeated. He squeezed through the

hatch and flopped down on Arkyn's bed. 'We're going to be allowed to join the hunt. But we have to hurry. The norwolf has been on the run all night.'

Arkyn hesitated. Was a hunt really happening? Was Dorregan really going to go after the norwolf? *His* norwolf. Arkyn felt his stomach tighten. Perhaps he should have spoken to his father after all. He should have told him what had *really* happened in the forest. He should have said that the norwolf had saved them, that he and the norwolf were… brothers.

He dismissed the thought almost immediately. What would have been the point? His father wouldn't have believed him. Worse than that, he would have laughed about it. He would have said something about the stories that children tell. Then he would have returned to his familiar habit of passing the day in near-silence, a brooding presence who seemed to have lost interest in everyone and everything.

Just then there was a heavy knock on his cabin door, followed by a deep voice.

'Arkyn…'

Arkyn froze. It was his father. 'I thought he would be asleep,' whispered Garran. There was a note of panic in his voice.

'So did I,' replied Arkyn, also in a whisper.

Hanserik Ironshield usually slept until the middle of the day. He spent his evenings at the firepit. He only returned home when the embers were cold and the pale light of dawn was spreading across the sky. The firepit was a place of talk and storytelling, but Hanserik rarely spoke. People knew that all he wanted to do was to stare into the flames. They understood why. Then he would sleep for a few hours before going out into the forest. Arkyn had no idea where he went or what he did, but the pattern was always the same. It had been that way ever since his mother had died.

Arkyn's bedroom door swung open and Hanserik stood at the entrance. He was a tall man with a thick mane of black hair tied at the nape of his neck. He was so broad that he almost filled the doorway. In fact, he had to bend his head beneath the frame in order to look at them both. His face showed no anger, but it was firm. It flashed through Arkyn's mind that he had never known his father to lose his temper. He had a sudden feeling that it was not something he ever wanted to see.

'You're up early,' he said to Arkyn. He nodded at Garran. 'And I see you have a visitor already.'

Garran bowed his head to show his respect. 'Good

morning, patron,' he said in a timid voice, which was the proper way to address a member of the Settlement Council.

'Morning father,' said Arkyn. 'I am sorry we disturbed you.'

'Actually, you didn't,' he replied. 'I wanted to talk to you.'

Arkyn was surprised. His father didn't like to talk unless he had something important to say.

Hanserik looked at Garran. Arkyn quickly guessed that his father wanted Garran to leave. He looked towards the open hatch. Garran stared blankly at him, then grasped his meaning.

'Oh,' he said. 'I'm sorry, patron. I'll leave you to talk.'

'No,' said Hanserik, raising the palm of his hand. 'This concerns you too. Listen to what I have to say, then you can go and tell your father.'

The boys looked at each other, puzzled.

Most men on the settlement were loud and aggressive. They used their voices like sledgehammers. Hanserik was the opposite. He spoke slowly and quietly. It was his way. Strangely, people tended to go quiet whenever he spoke. It was well known that a rowdy council meeting could be silenced by a few words from Hanserik Ironshield.

Now he sat on the stool by Arkyn's bed, his hands clasped

as if in prayer. He looked at both boys as he spoke. His gaze was steady. 'As you probably know, Dorregan has called a hunt.' His eyes settled more fully on Garran. 'He will expect you to join him, Garran. You are old enough now.'

Arkyn looked at Garran, whose cheeks had flushed slightly. Garran's eyes shone with excitement and he nodded his head slowly.

'As his Chief Counsel,' Hanserik went on, 'Dorregan will probably want me to join him on the hunt... and he will expect me to bring Arkyn too. After all, you're both old enough.' He looked at his son, his eyes giving little away.

'Yes!' Garran thumped the bed in delight. 'I told you, Arkyn. We'll go together! First blood… together. Blood brothers forever!'

Garran was almost shouting. His cheeks had turned bright red and he hd a fierce look. Arkyn stared at him, speechless. He felt his stomach turn. He had dreaded this. What should he say? He didn't want to go on the hunt. He *couldn't* go on the hunt. He had to find a way to stop it even taking place.

He turned back to his father. Arkyn felt that he had to say something now. He had to tell him about the norwolf rescue. Except that he didn't, because Hanserik's pale blue eyes were fixed on him, shining with a peculiar brightness. It was unusual, Arkyn thought, because so often his father's eyes looked sad, as if clouds had settled across them.

His father appeared to be studying him. It reminded him of the way Senni and Alys's mother would study the herbs stored on the shelves in her hut. She would run her fingers along the bottles until she found the one she wanted. Then she would utter the name of the chosen herb and you would know that her choice was final. There was no turning back. Hanserik's voice was the same.

'He won't be going on the hunt,' he declared. 'I won't allow it.'

***

Arkyn looked at his father in surprise and relief. Garran, of course, was incensed. He sat on the bed, his mouth hanging open. Eventually he turned to Arkyn. His eyes were wild. 'Aren't you going to say something?'

Arkyn lowered his head to avoid Garran's furious gaze.

'It's father's decision,' he said quietly, trying hard to look disappointed.

'Yes, but…' Just before, Garran's face had been pink with

excitement. Then it had turned pale with shock. Now his cheeks flushed pink again. This time with rage.

'But...' he said again. 'It's the wrong decision! It's not fair!'

'Just leave it,' Arkyn said. 'There's no point in making a fuss.' He noticed that his father was not looking at them. He had bowed his head and was staring at the floor. Arkyn realised that he would say no more. He was waiting for Garran to leave.

'Garran,' Arkyn said. He put his hand on his shoulder. Garran recoiled angrily. Arkyn was shocked to see that he had tears in his eyes.

'Leave me alone,' he said. He was almost snarling. 'You're not interested in hunting anyway. Ever since you rescued that norwolf pup you've been different.' He stared at Arkyn defiantly, knowing he had betrayed a trust.

'Shut up!' cried Arkyn. He felt sick. 'You're talking non-sense. You don't even know what you're saying.'

Garran reached for the sides of the hatch and started pulling himself out. 'It's just as well you can't come,' he said. 'You'd probably try and save the wretched beast.' He slid down the bank of snow outside the window and ran off. Arkyn was left alone with his father. The words 'you rescued that norwolf pup' were ringing in his ears.

Arkyn turned around slowly. His father was no longer staring patiently at his hands. He was looking directly at him. His bright blue eyes seemed to have darkened. There was a moment or two of silence. Not complete silence, though.

Arkyn's heart was thudding like a hammer wielded by a madman. He was convinced the whole settlement must be able to hear it. He tried to think of something to say but it was impossible. He couldn't organise his thoughts clearly. Finally, his father broke the silence. 'What norwolf pup?' he asked quietly.

Arkyn briefly wondered whether he should deny everything. Perhaps he could just say that Garran was upset, that he was telling tales. Perhaps he could blame it all on the storyteller's visit? He could say that the old man had put ideas into Garran's head. Could he talk his way out of this? One look at his father's expression confirmed everything. Only the truth would do.

'It happened last summer, during the early growth,' he said. Arkyn was slightly breathless, as if he had just climbed high into a tree. He paused and tried to breathe normally. As the words came, and the full story emerged, Arkyn slowly relaxed. His heart settled into its natural rhythm. It felt good to speak about this at last. Most of all, it was good to be able to tell his father.

'We guessed the pup was alone because we had seen the adult animal that the hunters had caught. They must have missed the pup.' Arkyn paused at this point in the story, as if expecting his father to ask a question. But Hanserik said nothing. He was listening in silence, his eyes focused and attentive.

Arkyn tried to remember every detail. He tried to describe everything truthfully. It felt like the right thing to do, particularly when the biggest and most important truth was not included at all. That the pup and he could talk to one another. But no one was going to believe that. Not even his own father.

He described how he carried the pup to Giant's Cave on his back. He told how Alys and Senni helped him nurse him back to health. He spoke about the night it returned to the forest, and about his fight with Garran. Then he was silent, waiting to hear what his father would say.

Hanserik leaned back, letting his back rest against the wall. He seemed far away with his thoughts. Arkyn watched him. He knew there was more to say, so much more, but something told him to wait. After a while, Hanserik nodded towards the open hatch where Garran had been. 'So Garran has said nothing about this to his father?'

'No, nothing,' replied Arkyn. 'But I know he thought it was wrong to care for a norwolf.'

Hanserik smiled slightly. It was a sad smile. One that seemed to be full of memories.

'Yes,' he said. 'That's what many people would say…'

Arkyn was watching his father carefully. He was wondering what he could be thinking. At last, he could bear it no longer.

'*Was* it wrong, father?'

Hanserik sat forward again, leaning towards his son. He reached forward and took Arkyn's hands in his own. Arkyn gasped with surprise. He actually giggled. Then he felt foolish for behaving like a child. But he couldn't help himself. It had been a long time since he had felt the warmth of those hands. They were so strong. And his father was looking at him strangely. It was as if he was looking right into him.

'No,' Hanserik said simply. 'It was brave.'

∗∗∗

'Arkyn?'

There was a thump on the outside wall of the shelter. Alys poked her head through the small opening, just as Garran had done a short while earlier. She immediately spotted Hanserik sitting opposite.

'Oops, sorry!' She pulled her head back quickly, bumping it hard on the top of the wooden frame. 'Ow!' She rubbed her scalp vigorously and mumbled her mother's mantra ('Down to the root, drawn to the leaf...') several times over. Slowly, she poked her head into the opening once more. Her face was flushed with embarrassment.

'I'm sorry, patron,' she said quietly. She spoke with her head bowed, avoiding eye contact. 'I thought this was Arkyn's room.'

'It is,' replied Arkyn. 'I'm over here.'

Alys looked up, puzzled. Arkyn watched with amusement as she squinted into the semi-darkness. 'Oh,' she said at last, turning towards the sound of his voice. 'It's so bright out here I can't see a thing.'

'What's up?'

Alys hesitated. She glanced first at Hanserik, then at

131

Arkyn. For a moment, she was lost for words. It was unusual to see Arkyn and his father together in the same room.

'It's OK,' Arkyn said. He glanced at his father. 'He knows about the pup.'

Alys stared at Arkyn in horror. 'He *knows*?'

'He does,' confirmed Hanserik with a wry smile. 'Although I think he's only been told *part* of the story.' Arkyn blushed as his father caught his eye.

'Still…' he went on, 'I probably know enough for now.' He turned back to Alys, his face rather cold and impassive. 'Shouldn't you be helping your mother look after your sister?'

Alys bristled, as if offended by Hanserik's question. 'I was with her all through the night, patron,' she replied firmly. Arkyn smiled to himself. He knew that it was never a good idea to question Alys's loyalty to her twin. 'She's sleeping now,' she added. 'Mother knows I have come here.'

'Why are you here?' repeated Arkyn, happy to change the subject.

'Because they are getting ready to hunt,' she said. She leaned her head further into the opening and thumped the outside wall in frustration. A light veil of snow collapsed onto the back of her head, but she ignored it. 'Dorregan is going after the pup. We have to do something.'

'I don't understand,' said Hanserik. 'How do you know they are going after the pup you rescued? It could be a different one. If one of the hounds has picked up the scent of an adult male this close to the settlement then Dorregan would be right to go after it. It would be too dangerous to leave it roaming near here.'

Arkyn hesitated and glanced across at Alys. She was still leaning into the window. Her cheeks and nose were bright red from the cold. Small flakes of snow had settled on her shoulders. She caught Arkyn's gaze and nodded. He needed to tell the whole story, or almost the whole story.

'We know it's the same one because we saw him again,' he explained. 'Yesterday... when the firehawk came. The pup chased it away.'

His father's eyes were wide in astonishment. 'Chased it away?' he said. 'You mean it deliberately protected you?'

Arkyn nodded, bowing his head, embarrassed. He knew it probably sounded ridiculous, but it was the truth. He didn't know what else he could say.

'I know it sounds impossible,' said Alys. 'But he confronted the firehawk and forced it to fly away. Then he stayed with us until we heard the barking of the hunting dogs. Then he disappeared into the woods.'

'That's when Niklas's dog picked up the scent,' said Arkyn. 'The pup had been with us, protecting us.'

'Well,' said Hanserik. 'A norwolf pup is not going to get far in a single night, even if it knew where it was going.' He leaned towards the hatch opening and offered his hands to Alys. She reached out to take them and shrieked with surprise when Hanserik pulled her into the room with one swift tug.

'Even Dorregan ought to be able to hunt down a baby norwolf.' He stood up. 'It sounds like we need to get going.'

Arkyn could scarcely believe what he was hearing.'You mean you'll help us? You'll help us save the norwolf?'

Hanserik looked at him seriously. 'I will. It sounds like you owe this animal something.'

'Absolutely,' said Arkyn. 'And besides, he added excitedly, we're….' Arkyn froze. He was about to say 'brothers' but stopped himself just in time.

'You're what?' asked his father.

'Nothing,' he replied quickly. 'I was just going to say that we're fond of him. I mean, after nursing him and everything.' His father was watching him closely. Arkyn felt himself blushing furiously.

'There *is* something you should know, patron,' Alys said.

Hanserik turned to her. 'What's that?'

'He's not much of a pup these days. I mean, he was at least as big as me.'

Hanserik smiled gently, warmth in his eyes. 'Still a baby then,' he said.

The smile broke into a huge, white-toothed grin. His eyes, too, were shining in a way that Arkyn had never seen before. Arkyn was confused. What on earth had got into his father? He had never known him to be so cheerful.

***

The rest of the morning passed quickly. Arkyn felt this was a good thing. There was less time to think about what was really going on. Less time to wonder what Garran might be saying to his father.

Of course, Arkyn knew it was not for him to say whether or not he should be allowed on the hunt. Hanserik was his father. A boy was bound to follow the instructions of his father. This was the way things were. But what about the wishes of a chief? Dorregan had wanted Arkyn to accompany Garran and Arkyn didn't like disobeying his chief. But there was no time to worry about that.

As soon as they had finished telling him about the young norwolf, Hanserik slipped out of the shelter. He didn't say where he was going. 'Meet me at the narrow gate in one hour,' he said, his tone serious. 'And,' he added, 'make sure you are warmly dressed. The weather is turning bad.'

Alys had hooted with delight. Arkyn knew she loved a challenge. He wasn't sure how *he* felt about another day trudging through thick snow. Alys was wrapped in several layers of thick fur. She looked as if she would have no trouble surviving a night in the Frozen Forest. It was not unusual, since Alys and her sister often slept under the stars while their mother picked and gathered in the woods. Survival in the wild had been part of their life since they were born. He dressed quickly and carelessly, wishing he hadn't forgotten to dry his clothes the day before, wishing that he had a mother like Tanita to remind him about such things.

An hour later they were at the narrow gate. Hanserik was already waiting for them. There was something long

136

and narrow strapped across his back. It was wrapped in a blanket and bound with twine. There was a second, smaller, bag too. Arkyn guessed it was about the right size for a bundle of arrows.

Hanserik led them through the gate and out of the settlement. Then they were running. Arkyn wanted to shout for joy because his father was leading him into the wilderness! They would track the norwolf together. He was certain that they would save him now.

They began at a steady pace and Arkyn found he could follow easily. He noticed that Hanserik was lifting his feet quite high and taking short strides. He moved smoothly and gracefully. Arkyn tried to copy him. It felt silly at first, like he was bouncing through the grass and snow. After a while, he realised that it worked well. It was important to move your legs quickly but the short steps kept you stable. He noticed that his breathing had calmed down. Behind him he could hear Alys taking short, grunting breaths, working hard to keep up.

'Lift your feet more!' he shouted to her. 'And shorten your stride.'

'What are you talking about?' she snapped.

'Watch me!' Arkyn lifted his knees as high as he could

to show her. It was too high, of course. He stumbled off the fresh trail his father had left and nearly planted himself face-first into a snowbank.

'Oh I see.' She ran past him without missing a step. 'I think I prefer my way if you don't mind.'

Arkyn brushed the snow off his leggings and set off after them. He no longer recognised where they were. He had assumed that they would take the usual path down to the river, which was the most obvious route towards the Frozen Forest. It was the path all the hunters used. But Hanserik wasn't using any known path, he was leading them directly away from the river, towards a part of the woods that he had never seen.

As they slipped between the first ranks of trees, the ground rose steeply upwards. They climbed through dense woodland. Arkyn was amazed how quickly they had gained height. Through a gap in the trees he caught a glimpse of the valley below. The river lay like a black ribbon, frozen and lifeless. In the distance he could see the settlement. How could they possibly have travelled so far, so quickly?

***

They came to a small clearing. The ground levelled slightly and a fallen tree suggested a possible place to stop. Arkyn was relieved to see that Hanserik felt the same way.

'We can rest here,' he said. He was barely out of breath, but there was colour in his cheeks. Arkyn also noticed that the black whiskers of his beard were flecked with ice. Hanserik swept the snow off the fallen tree.

'Have a seat,' he said to them. Alys flopped down gratefully. Arkyn didn't want his father to see how tired he was.

'Rest, Arkyn,' said Hanserik. 'We won't stop often.'

'I'm all right.' He walked to the edge of the clearing. He tried to look as if he was getting ready for the next part of the climb.

'As you wish.' Hanserik sat down next to Alys and opened the small bag he was carrying. Arkyn watched him closely out of the corner of his eye. He was hoping to catch a glimpse of an arrow or two. Instead, Hanserik pulled out a bag of nuts and dried mushrooms, which he offered to Alys.

'Hungry?' he asked Arkyn.

Arkyn wanted to refuse. He wanted his father to think

that he was tough enough to manage. But he hadn't eaten anything that morning and he was starving.

'No thanks.' He tried to ignore the rumbles of protest coming from his stomach.

Hanserik gave him a long look. He held out a handful of nuts.

'Eat,' he said.

Arkyn shrugged and took it. He sat down next to them and stuffed several in his mouth at once.

Alys smirked. 'I thought you weren't hungry,' she said.

'I'm not,' he lied. 'But we don't know when we're going to stop next, do we?' Alys grunted and took a sip from the water gourd she was carrying. Arkyn looked at his father who was chewing slowly, as if savouring each mouthful.

Occasionally he would glance down the hill behind them.

'What are you looking for?' asked Arkyn.

'Nothing in particular,' he replied. 'I'm just keeping an eye out.'

'Do you think we might have been followed by one of Dorregan's hunters?'

'I doubt it,' he said. 'Few people come this way. They all follow the hunting paths.'

'Why are we going this way then?' asked Alys. 'Wouldn't it be quicker to use the paths?'

'Easier underfoot maybe,' said Hanserik. 'But slower over time. And besides,' he added, 'norwolves travel in straight lines. Even your pup will do that. The hunting paths weave around too much, always looking for the easiest route. This way is hard, but it will get us to the edge of the Frozen Forest more quickly. If your pup is heading there too, then this is the way he will go.'

'But how would he know the way?' said Arkyn. 'He's young. He hardly knows these forests.'

'He would have been born there,' explained Hanserik. 'Even if the mother had been caught out here, she would never have had a litter outside the Frozen Forest. The pup will have a nose for home. He'll find his way.'

They were silent for a moment.

Arkyn continued watching his father, he had been hanging on his every word. He was doing that a lot, he realised. It was like a stranger had come into his life. This was not the father he recognised, the man who usually spent his days either sleeping or staring into space, lost in thought. He seemed younger out here. There was light in his eyes. He was alive and alert. Most of all, thought Arkyn, he seemed happy.

'And…' Hanserik continued. Arkyn noticed a tiny smile and his eyes glinting with mischief. 'We've been following his tracks all the way up here.'

Arkyn and Alys stared at him in astonishment.

'What? Where?'

Hanserik pointed to a patch of snowy ground.

'I don't see anything,' declared Alys. 'All I can see is mud and snow. Where exactly?'

Hanserik stood up and walked slowly to the end of the tree they were sitting on. He stepped carefully, as if he didn't want to disturb the ground. Then he crouched down. He made a circle with his hands and laid them down on the ground by his feet.

'Here.'

Alys grabbed hold of Arkyn's shoulder and pushed herself up, pushing him down in the process.

'Hey!' he protested.

'Oops,' said Alys.

She joined Hanserik at the end of the trunk and peered at the circle he had made.

'Oh wow,' she exclaimed. 'There really is something there.'

Arkyn stepped up onto the tree and tried walking along the beam of the trunk to them. He didn't want to look too interested. He leaned over them both, resting his hand on his father's shoulder, and looked down.

There were three, possibly four, smooth dents in the snow, next to each other. They were shaped a bit like tiny pears. Behind them was a larger smudge roughly the size of his fist. It was a paw print. There was no doubt about that. But of what?

'How do you know it's a norwolf?' he said.

'Well,' said Hanserik. 'It's definitely a wolf print of some kind. And if there are norwolves around here at the moment then it's very unlikely that common wolves will be here too. The norwolves would have driven them away.'

He got up slowly, taking care not to step on the print. He took hold of Arkyn's forearm to help him keep his balance on the trunk.

'It's quite a big animal too,' he continued. 'Not as large as an adult norwolf, but heavy enough. It could easily be the print of a male youngster.'

Hanserik pretended to push Arkyn off the tree. Arkyn yelped in shock, but saw the playful look in his father's eyes. The smile was different too.

In the years since his mother had died, Arkyn had grown used to a sad, weary smile that was willing to recognise joy in others but never in the man himself. But this was different. The sadness had been replaced by something almost playful and Arkyn was struggling to understand what was behind it, but he wasn't going to ask too many questions. He liked the way it made him feel, like hearing a song from a distant, long-forgotten land.

'You're good on your feet,' Hanserik said admiringly. 'Now, shall we get on?'

***

Then sound-storm began, a noise that only Arkyn seemed to be able to hear. He dropped down onto the log, clutching his head between his hands. How could no one else hear this? Even the forest seemed deaf to the chaos ringing between his ears.

He could hear Alys's voice but she sounded far away. 'Arkyn, what's wrong?' She was kneeling next to him, tugging at his arm. He was aware of his father too, but Hanserik wasn't saying anything. He was watching closely. Arkyn saw the look on his face: a mixture of wonder and... something else. Was it fear? Surely not. His father wasn't afraid of anything.

Arkyn groaned. This was worse than the last time, when the norwolf rescued them. And it was *much* worse than the first time, when he fell into the pit. It was sharp and piercing, it squealed and wailed. It made him think of the rats that scurried and scratched in the dark corners of the settlement. Then, almost as quickly as it came, it fell silent.

The voice that followed was old. It was soft and quite high pitched, and it was not happy.

You are wasting your time here.

It reminded Arkyn of Yasik, the elder who taught the children in the settlement how to write. It was the voice of someone who would be difficult to satisfy. Arkyn looked past Alys and Hanserik to the bushes behind them. There was nothing. He scanned the boughs and branches of the trees. Nothing. Hanserik had drawn Alys away. They were standing a few paces from him, watching silently. Arkyn stood up. He turned around.

Who are you? he thought.

The voice sighed heavily.

Such a pity, it said. *You don't even know who I am!* For a moment Arkyn thought that it sounded slightly hurt. Now that the sound-storm had gone, he was able to gather his thoughts.

How can I know who you are? I can't even see you.

Typical, the voice said gloomily. *Another one who lives through eyes alone. All hope is lost.*

What do you mean 'all hope is lost'? thought Arkyn. He suddenly had an awful thought. *Do you mean they've found the norwolf already?*

Is that all you can think about? You rag-eared pup! A missing norwolf is the least of my worries at the moment. It resumed the same mournful, gloomy tones. *All the good ones are gone. All hope is lost.*

Arkyn heard the voice first to his left, then to his right, as if the words were coming from several directions at once. He gave up trying to find it, instead he closed his eyes and focussed on what it was saying.

What good ones? he asked.

What good ones? echoed the voice testily. *What good ones, he wonders. I'll tell you about the good ones, young sprat. I mean the ones who see beyond their eyes and listen beyond their ears. The ones who stop running around long enough to watch the grass grow. Those are the good ones. You are up here chasing your norwolf brother. Hopeless folly, hopeless folly…*

The voice seemed to be drifting off, as if it were leaving.

146

Wait, Arkyn thought. *What do you know about my nor-wolf brother?*

I know a dreamer when I see one, said the voice. *And I know when a river should be left to follow its natural course.*

It was closer now, right in front of him. Arkyn opened his eyes but there was nothing. Hanserik and Alys were standing on the edge of the clearing, watching him closely. Arkyn felt the seed of frustration growing.

But I don't understand, he thought. *You're talking in riddles.*

Oh dear, oh dear, thought the voice. *So little known, so little understood.*

Well, thought Arkyn, his voice stiffening. *It's not easy to understand something when it's not explained properly.*

There was silence for a moment. Arkyn half-opened his eyes, wondering if the creature had gone. Then it was back. The voice was different, too. As if it had suddenly thought of something.

You do know that you're a communicant, don't you?

A what?

A communicant.

What's that?

There was a slightly wheezy squeal. Or was it a laugh?

Arkyn wasn't sure. Then silence, before… *Do you really mean to say you don't know what a communicant is?*

How could I? thought Arkyn, feeling irritated. *I've never heard the word before.*

Unbelievable… incredible… You have no idea? None whatsoever? It really makes me wonder… The voice faded as if it were drifting away, or talking to someone else entirely.

Arkyn suddenly feared that it was going to disappear. He wasn't ready for that quite yet. *Stop!* he called, trying to place the thought firmly yet politely. *Don't go yet. Just tell me, how do you know I am… what you say I am?*

There was a snort of disdain somewhere off to the left. The voice sounded exasperated. *How do I know?* came the thought. *Apart from the fact that I can hear you and you can hear me? And apart from the fact that we are able to have this exchange out in the open while your friends over there cannot hear a word of what we are saying?*

It softened and seemed to come nearer. If there was a form behind this voice, it was standing right next to him. But still there was nothing, only the words.

Oh yes, it said, much more quietly now. Close to Arkyn's ear. *You are a communicant. Most definitely. Listening and speaking with all living beings…*

There was a thoughtful pause. Arkyn felt that he was being checked over in some way, as if fitted for new boots. *Not that you seem very advanced… But you have the gift, no doubt – which is an increasingly rare thing these days.*

In fact, it went on, *you are the first communicant I've come across in a long time.* There was a weary sigh. Then the voice was gloomy again. *Actually, the vast majority of living beings neither speak nor listen these days. It's very quiet at the moment.*

Arkyn said nothing. He was turning the word 'communicant' over and over in his head. He had heard it before, hadn't he? Or something like it. What was it the norwolf had said? 'They communicate with all kinds of creatures.' His whole body suddenly felt hot. His head was spinning.

I'm afraid I don't know what you're talking about, he thought at last. He could feel the weakness in his voice, the voice inside his head. He was confused and afraid. It was too much to take in. *I only heard the norwolf. Nothing else has spoken to me. I'm not a commun… whatever you said I am.*

Only heard the norwolf, you say? But you can hear me, can't you?

Yes, but I can't see you.

Of course you can't see me, thought the voice. *You're not supposed to be able to see me… I'm a hedge-hermit. In fact, if you could see me then I wouldn't be a hedge-hermit. Or,* it added with another brief, sly chuckle, *I suppose you could be a hedge-hermit too.*

But I'm too young. I've only seen ten winters... I've never even been on a hunt.

The voice sighed heavily. *As I said before,* it said, *It's completely hopeless. Nothing is listening any more...*

Then there was silence. This time the voice really had gone, and Arkyn felt relieved, and strangely foolish. Had he just missed something really important?

'Arkyn!'

Hanserik's deep voice sliced through the cold air. Arkyn turned to where Alys and his father were standing. They were staring at him, eyes questioning. Arkyn stared back blankly. For a moment he couldn't remember where he was. His only thought was to find the hedge-hermit again. He wanted to ask more questions.

He felt an urge to leave his father and Alys, and it frightened him. He knew that he would never manage in the wild on his own. But the urge was saying, 'Leave them, you are not one of them', like an invisible rope that pulled him into the trees, over the next hill, beyond the valleys and out into unknown lands.

The dull thud of a snowball hit his chest.

'Arkyn!'

Flakes of ice and snow sprayed his face. Alys stood with her arm raised, ready to throw another.

'Stop it.' He raised the palm of his hand in surrender.

'What's the matter with you?' She was staring at him with a puzzled frown, as if she didn't recognise him. 'Why did you go so quiet? It was like you weren't here any more.'

'Nothing.' he replied. 'It was nothing. I was just… thinking.'

She snorted in disbelief. 'Thinking! Lost your mind, more like.' She aimed the snowball at a nearby tree and threw hard, hitting the mark with a satisfying splat of white. She pumped a fist and half-smiled. 'You looked like you were in a trance.'

Hanserik's face was more serious. The colour had gone from his cheeks and his manner had changed. The lightness and energy had vanished. He seemed wary and guarded.

'Sorry,' said Arkyn at last, looking at his father. 'I must have been dreaming.'

Hanserik walked back to the fallen tree and sat down next to him.

'That wasn't a dream,' he said. The bright blue eyes seemed to have turned pale grey. Arkyn suddenly felt nervous.

'What do you mean?'

'You know exactly what I mean,' his father said. 'You weren't dreaming. You were… communicating.'

Arkyn felt sick. That word again. 'Communicating?' he said, mouthing the word awkwardly. 'What do you mean communicating?' He didn't know what to say. He looked at Alys. Come on, he thought. You're usually the first to fill a gap with a joke or a stupid comment. Say something!

Alys was silent, staring at them both. She wasn't going to get involved.

'You were talking in your thoughts,' Hanserik went on. 'You were communicating with something. What was it? An animal?'

Arkyn stared at the ground. He felt as if he had been caught stealing or lying. This wasn't fair. He didn't choose to be like this.

'I don't know what it was,' he said at last, in a whisper. 'It's never happened like that before.'

'But it *has* happened before?' Hanserik reached out and

gripped Arkyn's arm. He wasn't hurting him, but the grip was firm. Arkyn could see the worry in his face: deep lines around his forehead and between his eyes, a hint of fear. Why? Arkyn wondered. Why would he be afraid?

'Arkyn.' Hanserik's voice was more insistent. 'When did this start?'

'In the growing season,' Arkyn said. 'When we found the norwolf. But I didn't start it,' he added quickly. 'It just… happened. I heard this voice in my head, asking for help.'

'You what?!' Alys dropped the snowball she was still holding. Her eyes were as wide as the moon. 'You can *speak* to the norwolf?'

'Quiet!' ordered Hanserik. He didn't shout but the tone was final, a command, in a voice Arkyn recognised but didn't hear often. 'Let him explain.'

'But I can't,' said Arkyn. 'That's just it. I don't know how it works, or why it's happening to me.' As he spoke those words he felt something rising from his stomach up into his chest. He wanted to reach out to his father. He wanted to hold out his arms and sob into his chest. He tucked his hands under his legs and stared at the ground. He took a deep, silent breath.

'I heard this noise in my head,' he said. 'It was terrible at first, deafening. Then it got quieter. Then I heard the voice of the norwolf.'

'And you were able to speak back?'

'Yes, but not out loud. It's hard to explain… I *think* what I want to say, rather than say it.'

Arkyn felt his father's grip relax. When he eventually spoke his voice was soft. It was almost a whisper.

'I don't believe it,' he said. 'A communicant…'

'*That's* what the creature called me,' said Arkyn. 'What does it mean? How do you know?'

Hanserik said nothing for a moment. Then he turned to face Arkyn again.

'I know,' he said quietly. 'Because your mother warned me you might be.' He smiled, but his eyes were full of sorrow. 'She was a communicant too.'

Arkyn stared at his father, speechless. And angry. Angry that he would mention her now, after all this time. Hanserik never spoke about his mother. All Arkyn knew was that she had died while giving birth. The baby, a girl, had died too. But even that he had only learned from others. Nothing more had been said.

A hunting horn sounded in the distance, its long, haunting note travelling up from the valley below as if looking for them.

Hanserik swore under his breath. 'That'll be Dorregan.' He picked up his bag and pulled it over his shoulder. 'We can't talk about this now. We need to get further ahead of the hunt if we are to help your norwolf.'

There was a brief nod to Alys before he set off up the hill again. Alys was on his tail straight away. She was like a willing hound. Arkyn's head was spinning. It was too much to take in. Finally, he jumped up and followed them.

***

They ran all day. At least that's how it felt to Arkyn. He and Alys were further from the settlement than they had ever been. The landscape was alien and strange. Every stream they crossed seemed a leap into the unknown. Every climb ended with an unfamiliar view. The world they knew seemed far behind.

From time to time, Hanserik would stop and study the ground carefully. Arkyn struggled to see what he was looking at. He seemed to notice signs that they could not. He never stopped for long, though. He would touch the snow lightly with the tips of his fingers or brush the side of a tree with the palm of his hand. On one occasion he even sniffed its bark. Then he would set off again. He was light on his feet. He never stumbled.

Arkyn followed in silence, wondering where this invisible trail would take them next. Whenever there was enough space he and Alys ran beside each other. It was comforting to hear her close by. They were breathing at the same rate. Their feet touched the ground at the same speed.

'What did you talk about?' she said suddenly. Her voice bounced up and down as she spoke. It sounded as if the words themselves were running.

'What do you mean?'

'That time when you were in the pit. What did the nor-wolf say to you?'

Arkyn kept on running. He didn't know what to say. He hardly knew what to think.

They jogged on in silence for a few more paces. Then Alys tried again.

'You must have been a little bit scared,' she said.

Arkyn couldn't let that pass. 'Not really,' he lied. 'I was just... shocked. I mean, I wasn't sure if the voice was real or not.'

'What did it sound like?'

'It was normal,' he said. 'It could have been one of us. I mean, it was a young voice.'

'So what did it say?'

'It asked for help, over and over again. There wasn't much else.'

'He must have been terrified,' said Alys. 'Stuck in that dark hole without a mother.'

Hanserik was only a few paces ahead of them. He wondered whether his father could hear them.

'You're quite similar then,' she went on. 'You and the norwolf.'

'How's that?'

'Well, you've both lost your mothers… And you're both comm… whatever it was.'

'Communicants,' said Arkyn.

'Yeah, that. So you have a connection.'

Arkyn thought about that for a moment. It wasn't a bad feeling to have. Something about it made him feel strong. But then he thought about the strange voice in the clearing – a pushy voice, angry even. It seemed to know things that Arkyn couldn't even begin to imagine. He pushed it to the back of his mind.

'It's like you were meant to find each other.'

'Maybe,' agreed Arkyn. He thought for a moment. 'One thing he did say…'

They had slowed to a walk now. Alys was watching him closely as they picked their way through the snow.

'What?' she said.

'Well, we saved him from the hole, right? And he saved us from the firehawk…' Arkyn hesitated. He was weighing up whether or not he should go on.

'So?'

'Well… he said there was a bond between us because we had helped each other. He said that we were like brothers in a pack.' Arkyn glanced at Alys. It was difficult to tell what she was thinking. He felt a bit silly and wished he hadn't said anything.

'That's it exactly,' she said, with a huge smile. Arkyn relaxed. He knew she would get it. 'You're part of the same pack!'

'Right now you're part of my pack,' said Hanserik, who had stopped just ahead. He had been listening after all. 'And you should come and see this.'

Hanserik was perched on a rocky ledge that seemed to lead nowhere. Just one more step and he would have been walking on thin air. Arkyn ran to join him. 'Careful,' Hanserik warned, raising an arm to block his way. 'You don't want to trip up here.'

They stepped up onto the ledge and looked over. He was right. Somewhere below them was the ground but you couldn't see a thing. The whole valley was submerged in white mist. Even the river – frozen solid and silent – was lost in the fog. They could still hear Dorregan's hunting horn, but for now its cry was distant and weak.

'How are we going to be able to stop the hunt in this weather?' said Arkyn. 'We can't even see where they are.'

'We don't need to worry about that,' replied Hanserik. 'Dorregan's a predictable hunter. They will cross the river below Bear's Ridge. Then they'll follow the hunting trail as far as the Frozen Forest.' He chuckled softly. 'Dorregan's horn may be strong but his hunting sense is not.'

'What about the norwolf?' asked Arkyn. 'Are you still following his tracks?'

'That's more of a problem,' he admitted. 'The trail runs

cold back there.' He pointed back the way they had come. 'I'm not sure where he went next.'

Hanserik leaned forward and peered over the edge. 'An adult norwolf would go that way,' he said. 'Straight over the ledge and down the rocks. It's the quickest route.'

'So you think that's what he did?'

'Possibly,' said Hanserik. 'But it's a tricky climb. If he's young I'm not sure he would be able to. He might have turned away from this ledge and tried to find an easier route.'

Hanserik studied the landscape for a few moments. Eventually his eyes settled on some dense woodland just below the ledge. A tree-lined ridge suggested a gentle drop down into the mist. 'He might have gone through there,' he said. 'But it would have been a bad choice.'

'Why?' asked Alys.

'It would take him back down to the hunting trail. He would be trapped in the valley.'

'So what do we do? If we don't know where he's gone?'

Hanserik turned to Arkyn. 'I thought you might be able to help us there.'

'Me? What can *I* do?'

'Maybe you could reach out to him,' he said. 'Tell him we want to help.'

Arkyn stared hard at his father. 'It doesn't work like that,' Arkyn replied. 'The norwolf needs to be here, next to me. I can't just call him.'

'Actually, that's not quite true,' Hanserik said. 'If you try, I think you'll find you can speak to him even when you can't see him.'

Arkyn bristled. Communicating was hard enough even when the norwolf was right next to him. How dare his father act like he knew all about it? 'How would *you* know?' he said, his voice quickly rising. 'You don't know anything about it!'

'I know a little,' he said quietly. 'From what I've been told…'

'By my mother?' said Arkyn. He felt angry tears welling up inside him. 'The mother you've told me nothing about?!'

Hanserik was silent. Father and son stared at each other for a few moments. In the end, it was Alys who spoke.

'Why don't you just try it?' she said to Arkyn. 'After all, it's what we're here for.' She sat down on the ledge, her legs dangling casually over the side. 'He might still be here somewhere. He might be wondering what to do.'

'He's older now,' replied Arkyn. 'He's bigger, stronger…' His voice trailed off. He looked at Alys, then turned back to his father. He was still angry. Even stronger than the anger, though, was a painful sadness.

'Why don't you ever talk about her?' he said.

'You were so young,' Hanserik said at last. 'I didn't know what to say to you.' He met his son's tearful gaze. His eyes glistened with sorrow.

'And now?'

Hanserik smiled gently. 'Even now it's hard.'

'But I want to know *everything*,' Arkyn cried. 'And I want you to tell me!'

Hanserik turned towards the ledge. He stared into the fog, nodding his head gently. 'Yes,' he said. 'I see that now.'

'Arkyn, look!'

About fifty paces away, sitting on his haunches and quietly watching, was the norwolf.

***

Why didn't you tell me you were here?

There is a hunter with you, replied the norwolf. His voice was different. There was a hint of mistrust, fear even.

That's my father. He won't hurt you. Arkyn looked back at his father. He and Alys were standing on the ledge, watching them.

Arkyn had felt a rush of anxiety when Alys first spotted

the norwolf. It had only been a day since their last meeting, but he was still surprised by the size of the animal. The tiny pup he carried on his back had become a powerful creature. Now that they were facing each other once again, the anxiety was gone. He felt peace, even joy. There was no chaotic sound in his head. There was only a gentle, musical murmur.

There are hunters looking for you, thought Arkyn. *You must get to the Frozen Forest.*

I lost my way last night.

You cannot go that way. Arkyn looked towards the ridge that Hanserik had pointed out. *It will lead you back down into the valley. The hunters will catch you there.*

Yes, said the norwolf. *And the dogs are faster than me. I am not sure if I can outrun them.*

Arkyn had no idea how to help. What had the hedge-hermit said? That it was 'hopeless folly'. Maybe the strange creature had been right. He took a deep breath. He caught the scent of the norwolf in his nostrils. It was a strong, pungent smell. Of course! It was obvious.

I have an idea, he thought. *I know how I can help you.*

How?

Your scent. The hunting dogs are tracking your scent. If we smelt the same, then maybe I could confuse them. Maybe I could lead them away from you.

But we don't smell the same, not at all.

We could, thought Arkyn.

He hesitated. Even though the norwolf was sitting on his haunches, he was as tall as Arkyn. Each paw was about as big as the boy's head. Arkyn took a small step forward. From there, if he wanted to, he could easily reach out and touch his long, broad muzzle. He studied the black fur masking the norwolf's face, looking for the eyes. After a while he could see them properly.

Then he was sure.

He didn't have to think. He stepped forward and put his arms around the norwolf's neck. He pressed the side of his head against the animal's fur and breathed deeply. The norwolf's fur was soft and warm. He could smell soil, wood, leaf, moss, stone. There was such richness in his scent. It was like smelling the earth itself.

Now we smell the same, thought Arkyn.

Arkyn took several long, deep breaths. He could hear the steady, powerful drum of the norwolf's heart. He could also hear Alys's silent scream as she watched from a safe distance. Arkyn smiled.

Pack brother, thought the norwolf.

Pack brother, agreed Arkyn. *Do you know what a hedge-hermit is?*

A hedge-hermit? No.

Oh. Arkyn was slightly disappointed.

Is it important?

Arkyn paused for a moment. Then he dropped his arms and stepped back. He thought about his mother. He wanted to tell the norwolf about her, but he didn't know what to say.

I don't know, he thought. *I don't think so. I just wondered…*

The norwolf stood up. Arkyn quickly took another step back. Once again, he found himself stunned by the size of the animal he had just held in his arms.

You will grow too, thought the norwolf. *You'll be as strong as your father one day.*

Arkyn laughed. *Maybe,* he smiled. *But I'll never be as strong as you.* He looked back at his father. Hanserik had sat down on the ledge. He couldn't be sure, but Arkyn thought he had seen tears in his father's eyes. Maybe it was just the brightness of the snow. He turned to the norwolf.

Where will you go from here? he thought.

There is a way just below the ledge where your father sits, replied the norwolf.

But that's dangerous, Arkyn replied. *He said it would be too difficult for a young norwolf.*

It is not so bad, replied the animal. *Your father is tall. Things look different from his height.*

There was a moment of silence between them. Then they heard the distant call of Dorregan's hunting horn. Arkyn felt his stomach turn. Time was running out. He thought of Claw leading the pack, and his mouth suddenly turned very dry. It was true that the dogs were only trained to hunt animals, but what would they do with a boy who smelled like a norwolf?

That worries me too, thought the norwolf. *They won't like to be tricked.*

They won't harm me. And my father will be with me.

He pushed the image of Claw's bared teeth to the back of his mind. Then he thought of something else.

Will you go to the people you spoke about? he asked. For some reason, Arkyn hoped that he wouldn't.

No, thought the norwolf. *I will go back to my pack.*

But you might see them, and speak to them?

I might, but they move around. They do not stay in one place like you.

Are they... communicants?

I believe that is a word they use, yes.

Arkyn stared at the ground, thinking hard. There was still so much to understand.

I must go, thought the norwolf.

Yes.

Arkyn kicked a lump of snow in frustration. He didn't want to leave now. He didn't want to face the hunting dogs, he didn't want to say goodbye again. The norwolf took a step towards Arkyn. His long nose nuzzled gently at the boy's shoulder. Arkyn reached out and put an arm around the animal's neck. He squeezed hard.

Pack brother, he thought.

Pack brother, replied the norwolf.

The animal loped across to the ledge where Alys and Hanserik still stood. He stopped nearby and looked at them for a moment. Then he turned away and slid down off the ledge. Just as before, Arkyn felt a powerful urge to follow. He wanted to leave the land he knew and go with his pack brother. He wanted to find these people who could also 'communicate' like him.

He also somehow knew that now was not the time. He watched the norwolf trace a path down across the rocks. The animal's movements were light and sure. No person could ever move like that, he thought. Then the norwolf was gone, his long white body fading into the freezing fog.

***

'This is madness,' said Alys. Her cheeks were bright red and she was gasping for breath.

They were standing on the valley floor at last, but there had been loose stones and patches of ice. Worst of all was the fog which had got thicker as they dropped down into the valley. By the time they reached the hunting trail they couldn't see much further than ten paces ahead.

'Really, it is,' Alys insisted. Hanserik and Arkyn exchanged a look, not sure which of them she was talking to.

'I'm freezing,' she said. 'We can't see anything, and you're pretending to be a norwolf.'

'I'm not,' protested Arkyn. 'I just want the hunting dogs to follow my scent. If we can lead them far enough in the wrong direction then the norwolf will be able to get away.'

He still wasn't sure what would happen when the dogs caught up with him. He was trying not to think about that.

'It's not such a bad plan,' said Hanserik with a reassuring smile. 'Arkyn doesn't need to go near the hounds at all. If they pick up his scent from here we can lead them away from the Frozen Forest. If they get too close he can scramble up a tree. Simple.'

They had been able to hear the hunt all the way down the climb. It wasn't just Dorregan's horn, now there were others. They could also hear the dogs. The pack was drawing closer. Arkyn was reminded of Claw and he felt weak with fear.

'Right,' said Hanserik. 'Stay close to me, both of you.' He set off, choosing a narrow path through thick woodland that Arkyn had not noticed.

He looked at Alys, whose eyes were bigger than ever. It was hard to tell whether she was scared or excited. He felt the need to offer her help in some way. Feeling clumsy, he stretched out his hand. Alys brushed it away and ran on, chasing after Hanserik.

'Come on,' she said.

Arkyn sprinted after her.

He was surprised how quickly the barking seemed to grow louder. Within moments, it felt as if the hunt was right at his heels. He glanced back from time to time, but could see nothing. He tried to guess how many dogs there were. Four? Five? Maybe more? It was impossible to tell. All he knew was that he needed to keep moving. The longer they could keep running, the greater the chance that his pack brother would escape.

And it was working.

They ran for an eternity. Hanserik led them further and further from the hunting trail, away from the path to the Frozen Forest, through dense woodland. It was hard to run without stumbling, but the dogs had picked up the scent. The sound of the hunt was right behind them.

'They're following,' Arkyn shouted. He felt both delight and terror. It was thrilling, but Alys was right. It was also madness.

'That's good,' Hanserik called back. 'Just keep moving.' Arkyn noted again how his father was running. He saw the way he lifted his feet and bent his knees. He moved lightly and easily through the undergrowth, like a deer. It looked so easy.

Neither Hanserik nor Alys heard Arkyn fall. It happened so quickly that he didn't even have time to cry out. One moment he was bouncing lightly over some broken branches, the next he was lying face down in a pile of mud and snow.

He rolled over onto his side and took several deep breaths. He heard was the dogs and they sounded closer than ever. He was about to shout for help but Hanserik and Alys must have run on, not noticing that he was down. If he cried out then Dorregan and the other hunters would be upon him. What would they do with him?

Arkyn clambered to his feet and sprinted as fast as he could. He kept low and tried to follow the route he thought Hanserik and Alys had taken. But he wasn't quick enough. The dogs were gaining on him.

Why don't you climb that tree?

Arkyn stopped.

'What?' he said out loud. He looked around. There was no one. Then he realised who, or rather what, it was.

The oak tree next to you, thought the voice. *You can climb that, can't you? Or are you hopeless at that too?*

Arkyn clenched his fists. *I'm not hopeless,* he thought. He grabbed hold of the lowest branch and pulled himself up. The bark was cold and slippery but he managed to gain a foothold. From there he was able to reach the higher limbs.

Not bad, the voice commented. *Keep going. They'll be here soon.*

I'm going as fast as I can. He scaled several more branches and then side-shuffled across to the trunk pressing his whole body against the rough skin. His heart was thumping wildly.

Right, came the voice. *Now, this is going to sound horrible.*

What is?

Arkyn's head was filled with a cacophony of screams and wails which seemed to flood the forest.

'Argh!' gasped Arkyn. *What are you doing?*

He gripped the tree tightly. The sounds in his head were awful, but the thought of Claw's teeth was even more horrendous.

Where are they?

They're sitting in a clearing about thirty paces away. I've told them to stop.

You've told them? How? Can you talk to dogs too?

Through the chaotic noises, Arkyn heard a heavy sigh. The sounds softened and grew deep and gentle settling into a slow, rhythmic pulse, before they stopped completely.

I can, thought the voice, *and a few other things too…*

Arkyn relaxed his hold of the tree, breathing more easily.

I still can't see you though, he thought.

Of course you can't, replied the voice. *As I told you before, you're not a hedge-hermit.*

Arkyn heard men shouting and orders being given. It was the hunt. He squeezed the trunk tightly.

The hunt is here. What do I do?

Your father is on his way to meet them. I'd leave it to him to do the talking if I were you.

Arkyn sighed with relief. My father… *Wait!* he thought. *You're not going to disappear again, are you?*

Disappear?

I mean… You left so quickly last time. I just… Arkyn hesitated. *I wanted to ask you something.*

What?

Well… He suddenly felt weak and tired. He didn't know where to start. Was the norwolf safe? What did it mean to be a communicant? Were there really others like him? Would Garran betray him to Dorregan? His head was crowded with questions, but there was only one that really mattered, a question for his father.

It doesn't matter, he thought.

There was silence. Arkyn heared voices in the distance but ignored them. He leaned against the tree and his body softened. He felt a gentle heat, as if now the bark was warming him. Just for a moment, it felt good to think nothing at all.

Much better, said the hedge-hermit. *Let's save those questions for another time, shall we?*

***

The hunt entered the clearing at a furious pace. Arkyn had slipped quietly down from his treetop refuge and crawled beneath the cover of some broad-leaf ferns. Dorregan rode at the head of the group, draped in the furs of a chief. He rode the chestnut mare, his favourite, a giant bearskin laid across her back. Arkyn's heart skipped a beat when he saw Garran follow on the hooves of his father, riding a grey filly.

Hanserik and Alys emerged from the other side of the clearing. Dorregan pulled up sharp, his black brows set in a grim frown.

'Hanserik!' he barked. 'What are *you* doing here?'

Hanserik ignored him. His face was creased with worry. His eyes darted everywhere. Arkyn guessed they were looking for him. 'The dogs,' he said at last. 'They…' But he stopped himself. The hunting dogs were sitting quietly on the ground, licking their paws and panting softly. A squirrel scurried up a nearby tree but they showed no interest. Even Claw was sitting quietly, waiting. In fact they all looked like harmless lapdogs.

'Niklas!' shouted Dorregan. 'What's wrong with the hounds?'

The young hunter took off one of his gloves and ran his hand along Claw's back.

'I don't know, patron.' Niklas looked at the other dogs. Two of them had stretched out on the icy ground and were dozing. A third was pushing its nose into the snow playfully. He shrugged his shoulders. 'I've never seen this before,' he said. 'They seem to have lost all interest in the hunt.' Arkyn smiled to himself.

Dorregan turned back to Hanserik.

'Ironshield,' he said. 'I was told you wanted no part in this hunt.'

'I am not here to hunt,' said Hanserik. 'I am teaching Arkyn and Alys how to track a tigerfox.'

Dorregan grunted. He didn't seem impressed. He glanced at Alys. 'From what I know of that one, she's better off mixing herbs,' he said. His eyes roamed the clearing. 'And you seem to have lost your son altogether.'

Hanserik hesitated, unsure how to respond.

'Er... Actually he hasn't, patron,' said Arkyn, emerging from his cover.

He stepped timidly into the clearing, aware that all eyes were suddenly on him. He walked up to his father and stood by his side. He also made a point of keeping as far away from the dogs as possible. He had to keep telling himself that there was nothing to fear. He wondered what the hedge-hermit had done, or said, to them.

'Arkyn!' gasped Alys in surprise and delight. 'We thought…' She glanced at Dorregan and promptly fell silent.

Hanserik was able to control his relief. He looked at Dorregan with no sign of emotion.

'The hounds seem to have lost interest,' he said.

Dorregan grunted again.

'It's the cold,' he replied in a weary voice. 'They couldn't track a frost bear in this wretched weather, let alone a norwolf.' He turned to his son, whose filly was standing quietly next to his own mare. Garran was watching Arkyn very closely.

'Another time, boy,' said Dorregan. 'We're not going to catch any norwolves today.'

Garran punched the top of his saddle with his fists. 'It's *his* fault,' he shouted.

Dorregan looked at Garran shaarply.

'What are you talking about?'

'He knows exactly what I'm talking about,' said Garran. He pointed a shaking finger at Arkyn. 'It's *his* fault that the trail has gone cold. They're not out here tracking tigerfoxes.

They were helping the norwolf escape!' Garran's face had turned bright red with rage and there were tears in his eyes.

Arkyn stood still, the colour draining from his cheeks.

'That's right,' said Hanserik with a broad smile. 'And the firehawks are flying us home.'

Dorregan chuckled. 'Now *that* would be a journey to remember!' he said.

'That's quite a tale you're weaving there, boy,' Hanserik said. 'Maybe you can entertain us round the fire at the next full moon?' He was smiling warmly at Garran, but Arkyn saw steel behind the stare. He was not surprised to see Garran bow his head.

'I… I just thought…' He looked up at Hanserik again, the fire in his eyes gone. 'Sorry, patron,' he stammered, 'I'm just upset that the hunt has failed.'

Dorregan laughed and began to turn his horse around. 'Come Garran, that's enough,' he said. 'There will be plenty of chances in the future.' Dorregan turned to Hanserik. 'Maybe the Chief Counsel and his son will join us next time. What do you say, Ironshield?'

'Maybe,' Hanserik replied. 'When the weather improves…'

Arkyn lifted his head just in time to catch the look that passed between Dorregan and his father, as if they shared a secret. Something that only the pair of them knew. The moment passed in a flash, but Arkyn was certain he saw it. Then he had an awful thought. Dorregan *knew*. Of course! That *must* be it. Dorregan knew about communicants. He knew about Arkyn's mother. He felt an icy shiver. Did he know about *him*?

∗∗∗

Little was said on the long journey back to the settlement. Arkyn walked a few paces behind Alys and his father, lost in his thoughts. He judged that the hunt would be back in the settlement by now and Garran would be in front of the fire with a cup of warm goats' milk. He recalled his anger, the tears in his eyes. How long would it be, he wondered, before Garran learned the truth about him? It felt as if more and more people were discovering the bond he shared with the norwolf. Alys knew. His father knew. Maybe even Dorregan himself knew? And then there was the hedge-hermit, who seemed to know *everything*. Arkyn kicked a lump of snow in frustration. He didn't want people to know. He just wanted to be back in Giant's Cave, caring for the norwolf pup.

Are you sure? Caves are so boring. Dark, cold and gloomy.

Arkyn wasn't surprised to hear the hedge-hermit again, he was just pleased it hadn't come with an awful fanfare of screeching. In fact he was starting to think that the hedge-hermit made that noise just to make sure communicants didn't ignore him.

You might be onto something there, thought the hedge-hermit. *Maybe you're not quite so hopeless after all.*

Arkyn smiled to himself.

So, what happens now? he thought.

You go home.

Isn't anyone going to explain any of this to me?

Not at the moment, Arkyn, no.

Arkyn was startled. *How do you know my name?*

I know quite a few things.

Do you know if the norwolf will find his way back to the Frozen Forest?

He will, replied the hedge-hermit.

Arkyn felt a surge of joy. He didn't understand how the hedge-hermit could know such things, but he believed him. He walked on in silence, following his father's footsteps in the snow.

It's not called the Frozen Forest, though, added the hedge-hermit.

What?

This 'Frozen Forest' your people always talk about... that's not what the people who actually live there call it.

What! he thought again. *What do they call it then?*

They have a much better name. Much more appropriate.

There was a long pause. Arkyn started to suspect that the hedge-hermit was playing games with him.

Tell me! he thought, as loudly as he dared without actually shouting out loud.

Winterscar, replied the hedge-hermit at last. *They call it Winterscar.*

Arkyn walked on, forming the word on his lips as he stepped through the snow. 'Winterscar,' he said. He glanced over his shoulder, looking back into the woods, back towards the place he thought was the Frozen Forest.

He turned back, focusing on the track ahead and the path home. The settlement was not far now.

So that's it? he said. *I just go home? It's all over?*

Yes, you go home, replied the hedge-hermit. *But it's not over. Not at all. In fact, this is only the beginning.*

End

Acknowledgements

With sincere thanks to everyone at Archetype Books for transforming a hazy pipedream into living reality.

To Marie and the pioneering young readers of Class 4, who sampled a very early draft and made enough encouraging noises for me to decide to keep going.

And to Jacqui, who is my beginning, my never-ending, and all my in-betweens.

Cover and illustrations

Ian Beck studied Graphic Design and Illustration at Brighton School of Art in the 1960s. He has illustrated over 140 books, mostly for children, and has written several novels as well as short stories and two collections of poetry.

ianbeck.wordpress.com

The adventure continues...

Follow Arkyn as he adapts to life as a communicant, where one wrong thought could put even his closest friends in terrible danger.

Pre-order your copy through <u>archetypebooks.net</u>

The Emerald Pendant

Arkyn and Alys were sitting on the edge of the signal platform, their legs dangling in the air. The drop beneath them was enough to kill anyone, but they knew the platform as well as their own rooms, every loose and rotten plank.

Arkyn could feel Alys's dark eyes focus on him. He had been dreading this moment. He turned to look at her. She was sitting bolt upright, her eyes wide with shock.

'You're joking, right?'

'No, not at all.' He turned away, unable to meet her gaze. He picked up a tiny stone and tossed it from the signal platform. There was a dull, leafy flutter as it landed on the forest canopy below. Perhaps, he thought, if he acted as if there was nothing more to be said, she would say no more about it. He dragged his hand across the wooden boards again, searching absently for another loose stone to hurl. She was never going to let this go. It was Alys, after all.

'You haven't heard anything?' she said.

'No,' he insisted. 'Nothing.'

'But I don't understand,' she said. 'After everything that's happened? Everything you've been through.' She paused, as if she needed a moment to understand what Arkyn had just said. 'The sounds have just stopped? Like someone has switched them off?' Her eyebrows folded into a confused, frustrated frown. 'It doesn't make any sense.'

'If you think about it,' said Arkyn, 'none of it made much sense in the first place. Maybe it was never meant to last.'